Power

The Power Series: Book One

Victoria Woods

Published by Victoria Woods, 2020.

POWER

First edition. November 18, 2020.

Copyright© 2020 by Victoria Woods

ISBN: 978-1-7361258-1-6

For Mr. V,

My real-life Shyam. Thank you for supporting my dreams and having more confidence in me than I do at times.

Prologue

Shyam

The basement of the warehouse reeked of mold and rusted metal. The stench of blood certainly did not help to quell the foul odor. I kicked the lifeless body splayed out on the discolored concrete floor in front of me. I wanted to make sure the motherfucker was truly dead—as if a bullet to both the head and heart hadn't been enough. We had already stripped away the prosthetics he'd used to disguise his face from us; he now lay naked on the floor like the trash he was.

Traitors like Vik were resilient. Like sewer rats, they always found a way to survive. Some would say that they were good at evasion, but I believed they were just pussies hiding from their imminent death.

A sole set of footsteps echoed from behind me. The sound ceased as another shadow cast over Vik's body, next to mine. My brother and right-hand man, Jai, had arrived. "Is he dead?"

"Where the fuck were you? Busy playing World of Warcraft again?" I asked in reply, my voice dripping with sarcasm. Jai was an IT genius, and he used that genius to run one-half of a tech company that bought up-and-coming startups that created data-tracking software. All these startups provided bits of information that we ultimately used to identify the locations of all other distributors, street sellers, and users. Sethi Tech was a front for our real business...the one that took place in dark alleys, night clubs, and rank warehouses. It kept the IRS and FBI off our backs. That was one of the drawbacks of supplying in the U.S., the fucking government, with all their rules and regulations.

"Fuck you, asshole. I got held up at the office. New acquisition," Jai shot back.

"Yeah, he's dead."

Jai took out his phone and took a picture of the corpse in front of us. I raised my eyebrow in question. "For our records," he said. I knew he had a good reason, so I didn't protest.

Vik had deserved to die. He had been sent by our rival as a spy and had disguised himself as an American street seller, using prosthetics to alter his facial structure so no one would recognize him. He'd paid off a few of our men to approve his background check, so that he could be supplied with product by us, and he had also managed to receive some insider information about our contracts with sellers.

His brother, Tarun, headed our rival organization in India. For years, our organizations had coexisted without any bad blood. It was a convenient situation. I supplied product to most of the United States and Europe, while Tarun's father had supplied his product to the greater part of Asia. Everything had worked smoothly until Tarun's father died and left operations to him. The son of a bitch was greedy and had one hell of a Napoleon complex, so it wasn't long before he broke the rules of peace and sent his bitch of a brother to divert business away from my organization. When my brother heard chatter on the streets about Tarun encroaching on our territory, I started tracking our new salesman using data gathered from various startups we had acquired. We watched his every move for the next month, just to be sure, before taking him out. When Jai analyzed the supply data, he discovered discrepancies. Deep down, I had been holding onto hope it was just rumor and that Tarun was respecting the invisible boundaries both of our organizations had established over the years, because killing Vik would start a war. But Tarun had started this shit, and I would have to end it.

Out of the corner of my eye, I saw a glint of gold below me. Vik's family ring, engraved with a tiger. How fucking cute and stereotypical. A Bengal tiger to represent their headquarters in Bengal. Jai and I had a Sethi family ring, too. Every major supplier family had one. We never took it off. It was another confirmation for me that our new salesman was related to Tarun.

Our ring was made of white gold but had an etched king cobra shaped into an "S," with black diamonds for the eyes. We were the true kings of the underworld, and it was time Tarun realized it.

"Cut the ring off and send it to Tarun's men." They'd relay the message.

I. Amelia

BEEP. BEEP. BEEEEEEP.

"Dammit!" I overslept *again* this morning—I had completely missed the first two alarms. If I was late to work, my boss would kill me!

I turned off the third and final alarm, still rattled from being jolted awake, then threw back the covers and ran to my shoe closet of a bathroom to get ready. I could barely move around inside without my legs grazing the toilet or bathtub by accident. The walls were off-white and in desperate need of some fresh paint. I imagined that it was once a bright shade of white, but over time the color had dulled. The grout between the white tiles on the floor was yellow with age and even missing in some spots. Much like the rest of my studio apartment, it was old and cramped. It was outrageous to me that *this* was what two thousand dollars a month could get you in Manhattan, but I didn't really have much of a choice if I wanted to be close to work. The proximity helped whenever I was running late, which seemed to be *always* lately.

I inspected myself in the mirror. The edges were cracked, but I could still see my reflection in the middle of it. God, I was a hot mess! I had stayed up way too late working on code again, and my face showed it. My hair was little more than a tangled auburn nest on my head, and the naturally coarse texture made it difficult to work with on a good day. The bags framing my dark-green eyes nearly matched them in color, and my skin was paler than usual. Even the freckles on my cheeks appeared dull. I really needed to stop working until the sun came up.

Out of time to beat myself up, I quickly brushed my teeth and washed my face. A shower would have to wait until after work. I ran a brush through my hair in an attempt to smooth down some of the frizz, then applied dark brown mascara and nude lip gloss. I threw on a vintage Blondie concert tee over fitted jeans. I took one more look in the mirror, then glanced at the clock and sighed—it would have to do. I stuffed my laptop and headphones into my bag and quickly slipped on my Converse. Then, after locking the door to my tiny apartment, I headed out to face another New York City day.

******

"Amelia! Where were you?!" Just as I'd predicted, my boss was pissed. Jason's face was fixed in a scowl as he stood in front of me, arms crossed over his chest. He was a short man with a thin build and thick-framed glasses perched on the bridge of nose. He was in his mid-thirties, yet his hairline was already receding.

"I'm so sorry. I missed my alarms," I said, apologizing earnestly as I slinked into my chair and unloaded my laptop from my bag. I tried to avoid his frigid stare as I powered up my device, praying that it would turn on faster.

"That's the third time this week!" Jason scolded me without any regard for my coworkers overhearing the admonishment. He seemed to be more irritated than

5

usual today, and I sensed it was more than just my tardiness. "I don't have time for this today," he said as he hovered over my desk, then he placed his hands on the tabletop and leaned in, too close for my liking. "I have a meeting right now. We'll discuss this later." Seething with venom, he lingered inches from my face, and I had to stop myself from gagging on the scent of his cheap cologne.

"Your ten o'clock is here," Tammy, his secretary, announced from behind him. Her voice startled Jason, and he snapped up straight and backed away from my desk, but his gaze lingered on me. I exhaled a silent sigh of relief as the space between us grew.

Behind Jason, I saw two tall men standing outside his office. One was dressed in a dark-gray suit, while the other wore a blazer over a black t-shirt and dark jeans. Their strong features shared a resemblance that indicated they were probably related. Both men had darker complexions and black hair, which made them look exotic. They were both handsome at first glance, but the man in the suit had more of an edge to him. His skin was the color of rich honey and he was taller than the other, though only slightly. His angular jaw had a slight shadow of stubble, which contradicted the rest of his polished appearance. His suit was fitted against his lean and muscular body; it was easy to tell he was in shape from how it clung to his tight body. His full lips were pressed tightly together, as if he were clenching his teeth behind them. However, his hazel eyes were the most noticeable aspect of his appearance. They were bright and piercing. I couldn't tear my eyes away from their blaze. They stared back at me with an expression so intense, I was almost scared.

6

Jason turned around. "Ah, Shyam and Jai Sethi. Thanks for waiting." He extended handshakes to both men and ushered them into his office. Before stepping inside, the taller man glanced at me once more. I squeezed my thighs together under my desk in reflex. Then the door shut behind them, extinguishing the fire that had burned a path to my core.

"Oh. My. God. They're so fucking hot!" Natalie was my desk neighbor and friend who had a keen eye for all things *male*. "I wonder what they're here for," she said as she let out an amorous sigh, leaning back into her desk chair.

Slowly letting out the breath that I had been holding during that heated exchange, I replied, "It seems like something serious, judging from Jason's reaction."

"I bet they're the reason Jason lost his shit on the phone the other day. I heard him shout things like 'takeover' and 'layoff' when I was about to go into his office to get his approval for the new implementation feature," Nat whispered like we were high-school girls gossiping during class.

"Takeover?" I questioned. "You don't think they're here to buy the company?"

The startup was relatively small and new. With about twenty-five employees including Jason, IP Innovations wasn't quite as green as some of the other startups out there, but we were by no means a huge force in the tech world yet. We had made a splash on tech blogs with our facial-recognition software, which could track the locations of people photographed by mobile phones. Facial-recognition software already existed but lacked accuracy for faces of women and people of color. The government had their own version of the software, but ours was the first with a ninety-seven percent accuracy rate. We'd formatted it for social media use, allowing platforms like Facebook and Instagram to recognize faces more inclusively. As a result, it would make "checking-in" easier for users and garner more ratings and reviews for local businesses.

Jason had even been interviewed for *Forbes*'s "30 under 30" list as a result. I guess it was expected that a startup could be bought if they produced successful products, but I hadn't been expecting it to happen to IP Innovations so soon. I had assumed that when the time came, a social media company or even the government would buy our feature and implement it.

IP Innovations had only been up and running for about six months. I liked the other programmers I worked with—minus Jason and his creepiness toward me—and the work itself. I liked it so much that I spent hours coding at home, sometimes well after midnight.

I dreaded being acquired by some enormous tech corporation where we would go from being people with names to just employee numbers. Programmers often lost their passion and drive when these mergers happened, since they were no longer a part of a small, close-knit team.

Nat's voice pulled me from my train of thought. "Well, whatever happens, I wouldn't mind working *under* one of those new bosses...or both!" She licked her lips in the most obscene way, probably playing out some sort of orgy fantasy in her head.

I rolled my eyes. "You have problems!" I redirected my focus back to my laptop monitor and started typing out code.

"No, *you* have problems, missy." She pointed a finger in my face. "You're like asexual! You barely even date. When was the last time you even got laid?" Everything was about sex and how she could get some in Nat's world.

"Hey! I *do* date," I protested. "Last week, I went out with that guy from the advertising company next door, remember?"

"Did you fuck?" she asked, raising an accusatory eyebrow.

"Oh my God, Natalie!" I prayed she would lower her voice before anyone else heard what we were talking about. "I'm not telling you anything," I whispered, hoping she would lower her voice to match mine.

Ignoring my hint, she continued at her regular volume, "That's because there's nothing to tell, or you wouldn't be so uptight right now!"

As much as I hated to admit it, she was right. The advertising guy was cute, but I was so bored at the bar with him that night. He kept talking about himself and barely asked me anything about my life. At one point, I gave up trying to participate in the conversation and instead planned out new coding algorithms that I could use at work in my head. I ended the night early and rushed home to code until four o'clock in the morning.

It wasn't like I was avoiding sex. I was not exactly a virgin, but my experience was fairly limited. I had given a blowjob or two and had some "okay" sex with past boyfriends. I hooked up with a few guys when I first moved to the city, but nothing ever lasted longer than two weeks. I had never experienced anything like the stories Nat would share about her escapades. She was a freak and was into really wild sex. The most adventurous thing I had done was give my high-school boyfriend a blowjob in the backseat of his car after we left the movies one night. To be honest, my orgasms came easier when I was left to my own devices—devices like my vibrator.

I found it difficult to find a guy who could understand my personality. I was an introvert, so putting myself out there and dating was not comfortable for me. The guys I did go out with took advantage of my quietness and overtook our conversations. I didn't think I was socially awkward, but I always doubted myself after dates. Maybe I really was the problem? Maybe I was sabotaging my sexual encounters, and that was why they weren't exciting? Maybe I wasn't capable of being adventurous in bed because I too much of a recluse? I wished I could be more like Nat—assertive and carefree.

Sensing my discomfort, Nat eased up on me. "Come on. Let's take an early lunch and check out that new taco truck down the street. Jason's not even going to know we left," she offered. I was relieved to drop the topic of my sex life—or lack thereof.

II. Amelia

Jason's meeting with the two handsome men had lasted well past when Nat and I returned from our two-hour lunch. After the men left, Jason seemed too preoccupied to resume scolding me, but his bad mood had continued through the day. He'd snapped at Nat for a minor bug in her code, then hovered over the other programmers' shoulders, nitpicking our work. Tammy, his secretary, bore the brunt of it. He'd had her running around the office, printing out documents and organizing them into manila files.

After Jason's outburst yesterday, I made sure to get to work on time today.

Now, it was a little before lunchtime, and the air in the office was still tense. Jason stepped out of his office and addressed us with his hands clasped in front of his waist. "If I could have everyone's attention. I have some news. IP Innovations has been acquired by Sethi Tech."

Sethi Tech was a giant in the industry. They were notorious for buying promising start-ups. Only the brightest programmers were hired to work for them. They usually required years of experience before even considering applicants.

This meant that the two men who were here yesterday were *the* Sethis of Sethi Tech. I didn't realize it when Tammy announced them, but now it started to make more sense. I had always assumed the owners would be a lot older and perhaps not as dreamy. They were probably playboys, since they had more money than God and were incredibly good looking. Women probably threw themselves at them.

Jason continued, "I was hoping that we could have delayed an acquisition for a little longer, until we polished our software, but the owners were adamant about making this happen as soon as possible. With that said, they want us to complete all code reviews and debugging of the new software by the end of next week."

Murmurs spread through the work area. "How are we supposed to work that fast?" one of our testers asked, voicing everyone's biggest concern.

"I realize this is going to put a lot of pressure on all of you, but I'm afraid we don't have a say in this," he said, shrugging his shoulders. "They want all of the code completed before some of you are relocated to their headquarters."

"*Some* of us?" Nat asked in frustration as she stood up from her seat. Apparently, the layoff rumors were true.

"Nothing is set in stone, but it seems as though they'll only be keeping a few of you on board after we deliver the final product and the merger is complete," Jason replied with a resigned look on his face.

Silence settled over the office. We all were mute from shock. We had poured our hearts and souls into this product. The office felt like a family. The idea of this team breaking up made my heart hurt. This software had quickly become a passion after I started at IP Innovations. If I were laid off, I would feel so lost. I could probably find a new job at a different startup, but I just felt like I wasn't finished with my role at IP Innovations yet. All of this made me feel depressed.

Jason wrapped up his meeting with us by offering more specifics on features that we needed to polish. There was so much work to cover and not enough time if we were to meet the deadline next week. Usually, mergers took months to be completed, so it was alarming that this was happening by next week. I did not know how we would finish the software in time, but it seemed like we didn't have much of a choice.

After Jason finished speaking, he disappeared into his office and didn't resurface for the rest of the day. The rest of us spent a good twenty minutes venting our frustrations to each other. The room was filled with hushed chatter. Eventually, we all recovered enough to resume working. I busied myself with my assigned features. If I were going to finish everything by next week, I would need to pull a lot of all-nighters. I couldn't waste any more time complaining about the acquisition. Every waking hour that I could work was valuable now.

At around six o'clock, Natalie pushed her chair away from her desk and massaged a kink out of her neck. My back felt stiff from sitting all day too, but I didn't have time to get up and stretch.

The office was still full, despite the time.

Nat stood up and walked over to my desk. Plopping her butt down on my desktop, she exclaimed, "Let's go get wasted!" My desk neighbors all looked up at her, annoyed that she'd broken their concentration. Nat either didn't notice or didn't care that eyes were on her.

I was glued to my laptop screen and kept typing furiously. "I can't. I still have so much more I need to work on for tonight." There was no way I could spare any time to go out drinking.

Not liking my answer, she slammed my screen down, shutting my laptop. I gaped at her. "What the hell, Nat?"

"No. If we're going to be working like mules for the next week, then we should have one last hurrah. Plus, after next week, we may not even be working together again." Her expression turned solemn.

That last part made me sad, too. It was a definite possibility that neither of us would be working at Sethi Tech. We would have to search for jobs elsewhere and be forced to go our separate ways. She was my best friend in the city, and the possibility of not seeing her every day formed a pit in my stomach.

I would probably regret giving up coding for the night, but she was right. We needed one last hurrah together before shit got real.

I scrunched my eyes closed, already remorseful of my irresponsible decision. "Give me five minutes to wrap up."

She pumped her fist in the air, bopping on my desk with excitement. "That's my girl!" she beamed as she added a shoulder shimmy to her bopping.

III. Amelia

Nirvana was packed. The club was overflowing with people swaying to the deep thumping of music. Beautiful women showed off their toned bodies while moving to the rhythm and grinding on equally sexy and firm-bodied men. The crowd thrashed us back and forth as we pushed our way through the dance floor.

Luckily, we had time to change our clothes before arriving. We stopped at Natalie's apartment to freshen up after work. I didn't own any clothes worthy of clubbing, so Nat was generous enough to loan me a form-fitting rose gold dress with the thinnest spaghetti straps I'd ever seen. It was too short for my liking, but she had insisted that it was appropriate for the evening ahead. She also loaned me a pair of too-high strappy black stilettos. As if the dress and shoes weren't enough, she did my hair and makeup too. I looked like a totally different person. My eyes were smokey and my lips were glossed in a rosy-pink color. My hair was set into soft waves that were still touchable and flowed down my back. I wasn't used to this version of myself. I'd never met *this* Amelia before.

Nat was perfection in her black-sequined miniskirt and silky top in the same color. She had long legs like a model and just the right amount of cleavage to fill out her top. She was always the first one noticed in a room, with her bright-orange hair and sun-kissed skin.

We made our way to the upper level of the club and found our other co-workers. Ramone, Dave, and Jen were already waiting for us at a table, drinks in hand. Nat ordered us all a round of shots when the waitress passed by. I wasn't much of a drinker, but I knew Nat wasn't in the mood to hear my protest. She was on a mission to let loose tonight and was taking all of us down with her, too.

"Can you believe that Sethi Tech bought us over?" Ramone shouted over the music. "I guess it was bound to happen eventually. The Sethis acquire nearly every promising startup."

Dave took a sip of his drink before replying, "I hear those Sethi brothers are into illegal shit, like drug dealing." Everyone stared at him, eyes wide with surprise. As if for effect, he took an even longer sip of his Jack and Coke, without offering any further information.

Nat punched him hard in his arm, mid-sip. He choked and coughed to clear his throat. "You can't just drop a bomb like that and stop talking, idiot! Explain yourself!"

Dave rubbed his arm while scooting his body out of Nat's line of fire. He continued, "Well, it's just that I heard some of my friends who worked at another startup talking. The Sethis acquired their startup months ago. They said that the brothers liked to scope out places that deal with tracking software. I assume it has something to do with keeping tabs on people who sell their stuff or their competition, if the rumors are true."

"So, our new bosses are drug dealers?" I asked in disbelief. What was I supposed to do with this information? I loved my job, but if I continued working there, I'd be involved in shady business too. Should I start searching for a new job out of principle? Maybe I would be a part of the group that got laid off, so I wouldn't have to worry about handing in my two-week notice to a bunch of gangster drug dealers. They probably did not handle rejection too well.

"Yeah, but those are just rumors," Jen said, trying to calm us down with her skepticism. "It seems a little unbelievable that drug dealers would be so heavily involved with all these startups without anyone going to the police. They've been acquiring businesses for a while. They would have been caught by now."

"All I know is what I've heard. That's all." Dave raised both his hands, signaling us to not shoot the messenger.

"Thank fuck! Our shots are here!" Nat interrupted. The night was finally about to start, according to her.

She grabbed the glasses off the tray before the waitress could do it herself and slammed one in front of each person. "Drink up!" Everyone downed their shots in one gulp, except for me. The smell had my guts churning. Nat grunted with distaste at my hesitance. Impatient, she suddenly pinched my nose and tipped the glass to my mouth, forcing me to swallow it. Warm liquid rushed down my throat and warmed me all the way to my belly.

She let go of my nose as I coughed to clear my throat of the burn. "Hey! I would have done it on my own!" I managed to sputter. I wiped the streams of spilled booze from my chin with the back of my hand.

"No, you wouldn't have, ya flake," she said and winked, flashing me her most charismatic smile. She was so damn pushy, but it was hard to be annoyed with her.

Then her eyes went wide as she zoned in on something over my shoulder. I turned around to see what she was staring at.

Speak of the devils—perhaps even literally. The two dark and presumably dangerous brothers were seated in a private booth near the balcony that overlooked the main floor. The taller one was wearing a black button-down shirt and dark-gray slacks that hugged every muscle of his frame. His sleeves were rolled up, showing the cords of veins in his forearms as he took a sip of amber liquid from his glass. He swiped his tongue over his lower lip to collect the remaining droplets of liquor in the smoothest of ways. His face was set in a stern expression as he spoke with his brother, who was again dressed in a blazer over a t-shirt and jeans. He was the more casual of the two, but still gorgeous. The pair of them attracted the eyes of every woman within view of the table, mine included. It was difficult not to stare at their chiseled features, which made them look like gods.

"What are *they* doing here?" I tried to keep my voice as low as possible, for fear of them overhearing.

"Oh, the Sethis own this club! Didn't you know?" Jen giggled at my doe eyes.

Of course, they owned the club. They probably owned half this town, with the amount of money they had.

Just then, two beautiful, leggy women approached the Sethis' booth with their arms slung around each other's waists. They seemed desperate for attention with how they slithered their bodies alongside the men in the booth. The blonde cozied up to the brother with the blazer. After an exchange of a few words into each other's ears, she slid on top of his lap, straddling him. He didn't hold back, either, making out with her right there in public. The blonde weaved her fingers into his hair, gripping him tightly. Her body writhed on top of the guy like she was humping him to get herself off. They seemed oblivious to anybody who might be watching, including the dark and brooding man sitting right next to them.

The brunette next to the stern brother threw her head back and let out a throaty laugh in response to her blonde friend's show. She tucked her body in closer to his side and undid the top button of his shirt before slipping her hand inside. I could tell from the way his shirt moved that she was stroking the bare skin of his chest. Unlike his brother, it didn't seem like he was enjoying the attention, because his lips were pressed tightly together and his hazel eyes seemed unaffected, almost bored. But he didn't stop her. For some reason, I wished he would.

His eyes were roaming the room, as if to find something more interesting to focus on. Suddenly, they caught mine. His eyebrow hiked up in curiosity, then lowered as recognition set in, but boredom no longer showed in his eyes. It was replaced by something more intense. Darker. He was daring me to approach him. My body felt it too. I uncrossed my legs and shifted one foot forward, as if compelled to stand up and walk over to him.

Brown hair came into view again, moving against his chin. The brunette must have sensed his distraction, because she tried even harder to get his attention. She pressed her too-big tits into his body and nibbled at his ear. His gaze never left mine.

As if his eyes were too bright, like the sun, I looked away. I could not watch the bimbo throw herself all over him anymore. I grabbed the shot nearest to me and slammed it down without hesitating or pinching my nose to mask the bitter taste.

Nat squealed in delight and clapped her hands. "That's my girl!" she shouted, then she grabbed my hand and dragged me downstairs to the dance floor.

IV. Shyam

Jai had convinced me to meet him at our club in the city to celebrate our acquisition of IP Innovations and discuss business. Even though I owned this place, I did not particularly enjoy meeting here to discuss business while desperate women threw themselves at me. My brother, on the other hand, lived for this shit. Planning and pussy.

I shouldn't complain, though. It *was* an easy way to score pussy. I never had to work for it. When I came to the club, the women lined up at our booth the moment we sat down. As flattering and easy as it was, I had real business to discuss tonight. *Tarun.*

"Any word from India?" I surveyed my surroundings as I took a sip of my scotch. I was always aware of the room around me. Always on guard. Enemies waited until you were distracted to strike. Though, they wouldn't be dumb to attack me in my own club. This place was teeming with my men, all armed and ready to kill. To the untrained eye, they just seemed like terrifying bouncers.

"Nothing yet. Tarun's been quiet for too long," Jai replied, eyeing a tall blonde at a table across the room. He flashed her a mega-watt smile as an invitation to join him. "You think he saw Vik's ring yet?"

"Yes, he's seen it." I was sure of it. Tarun's only brother was dead. We were Indian, and family loyalty ran deep for us. Vik died serving his brother, and in return, Tarun

22

would do anything to avenge his death. He was most likely quiet because he was plotting his next move.

The blonde who'd been making eyes at Jai sauntered up to our booth with a friend attached to her hip. "You boys want to buy us a drink?" the blonde asked sheepishly as she batted her eyelashes.

I glared at her in annoyance. We should have met at our suite upstairs to avoid this shit. I wasn't in the mood for easy pussy when I had a war to plan.

"Lighten up, man. Have a little fun. We just acquired a company with the best tracking software available. We should be celebrating. Instead, you're dressed like you're headed to the office." Jai motioned for the blonde to join us. Her presumptuous friend assumed the invitation extended to her as well and slid into my side of the booth, pressing her thin body tightly against my frame.

While Jai and the blonde dry humped each other next to me, the brunette took it upon herself to undo my top button and stroke my chest. The hairs on my body stood up—but not from the woman touching me. I felt like I was being watched.

I surveyed the room until my eyes met with a pair of green ones. I remembered those eyes. They held my attention just like the last time I saw them. Though their owner, my new employee, looked different from the last time I saw her. She looked sultry in that little dress. Her fair skin was flushed, and I could tell her breathing had sped up by the way her chest rose and fell so quickly. My gaze slid down to her breasts, where I could see her nipples poking through the thin fabric of her dress. *No bra.* A devious smile spread across my lips at this discovery.

I had completely forgotten about the woman groping my chest until I felt her teeth graze my ear lobe. The fair angel across the room huffed in irritation, and her neck turned bright red before she slammed a shot and stormed off. I knew that look. She was jealous. I smirked to myself—perhaps tonight was going to be interesting, after all.

V. Amelia

I threw myself into the beat of the music on the dance floor, trying to wipe away the image of Miss Big-Tits groping my new boss. It wasn't long before the vibe got to me. I felt sexy in my skimpy dress and let loose, shaking my hips and dipping low to the ground.

I worked up a hard sweat from all the dancing. Nat and I made frequent stops at the bar to hydrate, drinking shots like water. This was the most alcohol I'd ever drunk in one night.

I didn't know why I had been so bothered earlier. I told myself that it was probably just because I was disturbed that my new boss was so unprofessional, letting random women fondle him in public where his employees could see. Sure, he didn't know we would be there, but it was a public place, so really anyone could see. And he did own the club, so it was even more sleazy that he would act that way in his own establishment.

Working for that horny drug dealer now seemed to be out of the question. I had morals, and I hadn't studied so hard in college to work for someone as tacky as him. Jason had been bad enough with his creepiness, but this crossed a line. I should email my resignation and quit immediately!

After what felt like hours of dancing and drinking, I felt my brain getting fuzzy. I needed to take a breather. All the alcohol and hot bodies nearby were suffocating me. I signaled to Nat that I was going to find a bathroom.

She gave me the thumbs up and continued grinding on some random guy that had bought us our last round of drinks.

I pushed my way through the crowd and held on carefully to the stairway railing as I wandered back up to the second floor. My feet were killing me because they weren't used to heels. I would have killed for my sneakers right now.

Finding myself in a long, narrow hallway, I assumed the bathroom was at the far end, and I made my way further down in search of it. It seemed too quiet to be the way to the restroom, though. There should have been a ton of people hanging around here.

I realized only too late that I wasn't alone. A large, cold hand covered my mouth from behind, while another wrapped around my waist too tightly. My back was pressed against something hard. I tried to scream, but no sounds escaped from my covered mouth. Hot breath wafted over the side of my neck.

"Don't move, bitch," a deep warning rang through my ear. My chest started heaving in panic. God, why did I think it was a good idea to wander around the club alone?

With one quick move, I was slammed up against the wall. His hand squeezed my neck, holding me in place and making it difficult to breathe. My head buzzed from the force of the impact and lack of oxygen.

As my vision refocused, I saw the dark shadow of a person looming over me. His eyes were difficult to see under his baseball cap, but his mouth was fixed into a cocky grin, like a hyena about to pounce.

"Looks like I got lucky this time. You're a pretty one, aren't ya?" he hissed in my face.

His head tipped down slowly, until he was looking directly at my chest. I winced as his rough, clumsy hand squeeze one of my breasts.

"Too bad these tits are natural. I'm usually into something bigger," he sneered. "They will have to do."

Tears leaked from the corners of my eyes. His body was so close to mine that I could feel his disgusting dick press into my belly. My stomach churned. I was going to vomit.

In a flash, the pressure on my throat was gone. I slid to the floor, coughing and gasping for breath. I saw my assailant on the ground.

Standing over him was my new boss. His body was stiff with rage as he aimed a gun at the fallen man. The veins in his forearms protruded with tension as he gripped the weapon in his hand. He handled it with such familiarity, it was more like a natural extension of his arm.

"If I ever see you in my club again, I won't hesitate to put a bullet in your head." He kept his voice low, but it terrified me more than my attacker's had.

The man on the floor started to crawl to get away. As if it were not fast enough for his liking, my boss smacked him in the back of the head with the barrel of his gun. The man bolted out of the hallway as fast as he could.

I was left alone with a new figure towering over me. A true predator. I didn't speak for fear of his wrath. His eyes bore into mine as I crouched on the floor, peering up at him.

"Get up," he barked at me.

I was frozen to the ground. Impatience radiated from him. He grabbed me firmly by my arms and righted me against the wall. I was probably over five-foot-seven with my stilettos, but he was still taller than me. His fingers dug into my skin, keeping me from moving away.

The fire in his eyes from earlier had not dimmed. It seemed even stronger now as they studied my face. I held my breath as his gaze roamed down to my lips. I parted them, but no air escaped.

Suddenly, his gaze flicked to my neck. His jaw clenched in rage—my attacker must have left marks on me. His fingertips touched my skin softly, tracing what he saw.

Unintentionally, I sighed out the breath I had been holding in all this time, and it came out as a soft moan. Those eyes flashed back to mine with a wild and hungry expression.

He shifted his body closer. He was so near that I could smell his essence—leather and tobacco. His fingers slid down my body to my waist, where they held me in place. I couldn't run away if I wanted to, even though I knew I should. This man was dangerous. I could feel it in the way he looked at me, like he could ruin me.

His hard cock pressed into my lower belly. Without thinking, I tilted my pelvis to meet him. I needed friction to ease the ache between my legs. He ground his dick further into me, as if reading my mind. God, it felt good.

My back arched off the wall as my head fell back in pleasure. I needed more.

I lifted my knee to his hip so I could wrap my leg around his ass, giving him more access to my most sensitive area.

Suddenly, he pushed my leg down and released his grip on me. I blinked up at him in confusion. He stepped backward, away from me. His eyes grew cold, the fire extinguished. *Why is he upset with me?*

My cheeks heated with the shame of rejection. I crossed my arms over my chest to keep from feeling exposed.

"Go home." His voice was low and steady, as if nothing had happened.

I stood there, doe-eyed, unable to move or speak. He took one more glance at me before walking away.

Just like that, I was alone—wet and rejected.

VI. Amelia

The next morning was brutal. I had tossed and turned in bed all night, despite needing sleep to cure my hangover.

My eyes were puffy, and bruises had formed on my neck from the assault the night before. I had them covered up with a scarf to avoid any probing questions from my coworkers. Thank God it was Friday, and I could catch up on sleep this weekend.

I was miserable. I had the biggest migraine from drinking too much. I felt nauseous about almost being raped by some ogre and embarrassed with how I threw myself at my new boss. The last part disturbed me the most because I was not *that* girl. I didn't grind on random guys, let alone alleged drug dealers, in dark hallways of clubs.

Ugh. It sounded even worse the more I thought about it.

Thankfully, I was able to keep my mind busy by writing and polishing code all morning. Nat must have been feeling like crap too because she barely spoke to me when she trudged into the office. Most of her responses to coworkers came out as incoherent mumbles.

Jason called for our attention just before lunchtime. I glanced up from my monitor at the sound of his voice. *Shit!*

He was standing right next to Jason. Dressed in a navy suit and black tie, he looked fresh and polished, as if he hadn't had me pressed up against a wall just last night. Meanwhile, I had stumbled into the office with ripped jeans and a Pink Floyd concert t-shirt. I tucked my scarf closer to my neck for comfort.

"I'd like to introduce you all to one-half of Sethi Tech, Mr. Shyam Sethi." Jason gestured to Mr. Tall-Dark-and-Sexy enthusiastically.

Shyam. I hadn't known which brother he was up until now. And now that I'd heard his name, it made sense. It suited him. Strong and mysterious.

"Mr. Sethi is here to see the progress we've made," Jason continued. "Shyam, would you like to say a few words?"

It was difficult to read Shyam's expression. He didn't seem angry, but perhaps he was irritated to be here.

"Thank you, Jason," he began. "I would like to commend all of you on your hard work."

This was the first time I had heard him speak more than two words. His tone was business-like, yet deep and dangerous. And he didn't have an American accent, but it wasn't quite Indian either. It was more British, I supposed. Whatever it was, it made me feel that familiar tingle between my legs when I heard it. Why did he have this effect on me?

"Asking you to complete this project in a limited amount of time is not ideal," he continued, "but it is necessary. For this reason, I will be meeting with each of you individually today to discuss your progress." His gaze settled on me when he said that last part.

I panicked and diverted my gaze down to my shoes to avoid his penetrating stare.

"Please be prepared to present your features in a concise manner," Jason interrupted. Shyam tightened his jaw, most likely because he didn't appreciate being cut off.

"Shyam, if you'll follow me, I'll show you to the conference room." Jason ushered him away.

Great. First, he rubs his dick against me and then turns me away. Now, I have to be alone with him to bask in my humiliation. I should have called in sick.

******

It was late and I had yet to be called in to present. I tried to focus on the task at hand and rehearse all the specifications I had worked on in my head to calm my nerves. If I took my focus away from presenting to Shyam and just concentrated on the work, then I would be okay.

It was a little after six-thirty and I was the last one in the office. I assumed Jason had left too, since the lights in his office were turned off.

Dave came out of the conference room and collected his laptop and bag. "Good luck," he said as he headed out the door.

It was my turn. I stood up and gathered my laptop. I walked slowly to the conference room, praying my feet would get me there even though they felt like running away. When I reached the door, I raised my fist to knock before entering.

"Come in," Shyam's voice echoed through the door before I had the chance.

I followed his order. The privacy blinds had been drawn to prevent anyone from seeing into the room. It was intimidating to be in here with no view of the desks and chairs beyond the windows.

Shyam sat with perfect posture at the head of the table. He gestured to the opposite end and commanded, "You may begin, Ms. Becker."

I took a deep breath to steady my shaky legs as I approached the front of the room. My stomach was filled with butterflies.

I connected my laptop to the screen projector on the wall and pulled up the app onto my screen. All the while, he sat focused on me, with one arm across his chest and the index finger of his other hand pressed against his lips. A silver ring flashed on his finger as he waited for me to start.

I cleared my throat and willed myself to speak. *Just focus on the work.* "Most tracking data collected from various apps collect bits of information, like a person's name or username. For example, Facebook will collect information that is entered, like a username and phone number, and associate it with a specific account. Facial-recognition software offers another dimension to collecting data. When users upload photos to any app, we can use the embedded coordinates of where the photo was taken to ask the user to check in to certain locations or rate and review local businesses where the photo was taken. But I'm sure you know this already." I realized this was all probably redundant for him.

He dropped his finger from his mouth and leaned back in his chair. "I do. How is what you've done different from what is currently available?"

"Most facial-recognition software uses special algorithms to identify a person from certain traits specific to their face. However, the software that already exists is only specific to a certain type of demographic."

"Caucasian men," he added.

"Yes. Specifically, Caucasian men over the age of forty. Available software suffers from large margins of error when trying to identify other races or women. Our software has the highest accuracy available for identifying demographics other than older white men." Speaking about what I knew was a lot easier than I had feared. It helped to ease my nerves.

"Would someone be able to trick your software from identifying them accurately?"

The short answer was *no*. But I wasn't sure why someone would try to trick the software. It was meant for social media use.

"Cloaking" was used to hide from facial-recognition software. It involved changing pixels of an image to trick the software, though the cloaked image remained virtually indistinguishable from the original image to the naked eye. A person could use cloaking software to alter their facial features in pictures. Many of those altered pictures would be uploaded and linked to a particular person, thus preventing facial-recognition software from "accurately" identifying a person when a real photo was uploaded. The government had their own version of facial-recognition software that was unaffected by cloaking. Ours was the first facial-recognition software meant for social media use that was also unaffected by cloaking.

I had implemented a feature that could cloak any image of a person, so that if a person tried to cloak their own photo, our software would have already altered the uploaded image, beating the person to the punch. It would use various combinations of the cloaked images it generated to identify a person who was trying to hide their identity.

Shyam slowly stood up from his chair. I hadn't even answered his question yet, so I wasn't sure what this meant. I stopped talking as he stalked toward me like a panther, his strides quiet but ready to pounce at any moment.

I turned to face him when he reached my side. He turned me back to my original position, facing the conference table. I felt warm hands inch the hem of my shirt up, exposing my midsection. Goosebumps spread all over my body.

"Go on," he whispered in my ear from behind. His breath caressed my sensitive skin.

Still unsure, I kept talking. "No...our software is still...able to accurately identify people...even if cloaking is used." My voice came out between panting breaths.

One of his hands rested on my waist, as the other pushed on my upper back until my chest met the surface of the table. I turned my head back to see him standing behind me with a satisfied look on his handsome face. He pressed my face down on its side so I couldn't see him anymore.

"And how did you do that?" he growled as he stroked my belly.

It was getting more difficult to concentrate on my presentation. My body was on fire with anticipation. "A built-in feature," I managed to say.

His hand roamed from my belly to the button at the top of my jeans. With steady fingers, he undid it and lowered my zipper ever so slowly. Oh God, what was he doing?

"What kind of feature?" he asked. I felt him move in closer to me, so his cock was pressed against my ass through my jeans. His hand moved under the waistband of my panties and grazed the scant amount of hair that I kept there.

"One that could...cloak images...*for* reference," I managed to say. I didn't know how I could keep talking at this rate. I was so needy that my pussy ached.

"You're a smart girl," he said as he slid his hand lower and found my clit. I couldn't hold back the moan that escaped my lips. I knew he heard it too, because his cocked jerked against my ass.

"*Bolo*," he said gruffly in Hindi. *Tell me.* "Can this be used to find the location of a person?" His fingers rubbed a single tight circle on my clit. My body jolted with pleasure from his brief touch. He weaved his free hand into the hair on the back of my head and held me in place. His dominance satisfied me.

He continued massaging my clit. My palms pressed into the table in front of my head. My panties were so wet that they slid against my swollen flesh.

"Yes," was the only answer I could manage. Pleasure was building. His fingers moved faster, applying more pressure. I was almost there. I felt like I would die if he stopped.

"And there is no way to block the integrated cloaking feature?" he asked gruffly as he rubbed his dick against my ass. It was all too much. I couldn't answer. I was ready to burst.

He grew impatient when I didn't answer him and stilled his hand. I cried out in frustration.

He yanked on my hair to turn my head to face him, and I yelped at the pain. "*Bolo*, Ms. Becker." His eyes were full of force.

"No," I blurted, "there is no way to block it."

"At all?" he demanded as he pulled my hair harder.

"Only if someone physically altered their appearance," I answered quickly, desperate for him to continue stroking me.

He seemed happy with this answer and loosened his hold on my head. He didn't force my face down to the table again. Instead, his fingers worked faster on my clit, bringing me back to my threshold. Then he slipped a finger inside. "Oh God!" I moaned.

"Come for me," he growled.

As if he owned it, my body responded automatically. I detonated under his fingertips as I cried his name out. "Shyam!"

My torso collapsed onto the table as my orgasm washed over me. I took a few moments to catch my breath.

Shyam pulled away from my body. I pushed myself up off the table and saw that he had made his way to the door. He was about to step out and leave me—again.

"Shyam!" I raised my voice at him in anger. I was usually soft-spoken, but I was furious that this was happening again. The first time, I had been pissed at myself, but this time, I was pissed at him.

He turned back toward me with an unreadable expression on his face.

The scarf around my neck had come undone during his manhandling. His eyes flicked to the bruises on my skin. It almost seemed like concern entered his eyes. Before I could ask him what was wrong, he stepped out the door and closed it behind him.

VII. Shyam

Smoke trailed from the end of my cigar. I brought it to my lips and inhaled deeply. Tipping my head back, I exhaled slowly, letting the tension in my shoulders release.

Nirvana was full of life tonight. Fridays were always good. The women were out in droves.

Jai and I sat in my private office suite on the third floor. One wall was made of tinted glass—bulletproof and soundproof—and overlooked the entire club. Below us, I could see hordes of horny twenty-year-olds looking to hookup. They were young, with tight asses and perky tits, and danced for attention—to be noticed by young guys looking for an easy fuck.

My mind wandered to Amelia as I breathed in another puff from my cigar.

Amelia Anne Becker, age twenty-three. Only child of Joseph and Angela Becker from Seattle, Washington. Her father had been an electrician, and her mother was a nurse. Joseph Becker died from cancer when Amelia was fifteen. She had lived with her mother until she moved across the country to enroll in NYU's School of Engineering on a scholarship. She'd graduated with a bachelor's degree in computer science and held top honors.

She had been active in many engineering organizations in university and had won awards for a few competitions. Her professors described her as "bright" and "driven." IP Innovations was her first job out of school.

Her record was clear. No misdemeanors, or even parking tickets. She had dated sporadically since moving to the city, but nothing serious to note.

She was squeaky clean. Innocent...almost virginal, even. Her file said that she had visited a gynecologist nearby and had an active prescription for birth control that was renewed monthly, despite not dating regularly.

I liked women with experience. Virgins needed to be broken in before they learned to fuck well. The risk of them becoming too attached was high. I enjoyed my share of them, but nothing could compare to a woman who knew her way around a dick.

Amelia looked like a virgin on the outside, but when I took control of her, she knew exactly how to respond. She wasn't afraid to want more. I had not planned on touching her again today at the office, but after cornering her at the club, I couldn't resist. Something drew me to her whenever she was near.

When I found her being mauled by that motherfucker, I saw red. Rage took over and I wanted to beat the shit out of him. Then, when she stared at me with that innocent look, I needed to erase any evidence that someone else had touched her first.

Fuck, her skin was so soft, and my dick liked it. Having her bent over the conference table just a few hours ago had unleashed something primal in me. Hearing her call my name while she came had awakened something in me that I had not felt with other women. And she was intelligent. The way she spoke about her work turned me on. I was not used to women talking about something other than how they wanted to suck me off.

Jai sat back in the leather armchair across from me, enjoying his cigar while he checked out the view below us.

"Our guys found Manish's body," Jai said between exhaling rings of smoke from his mouth.

"Where?" I could feel my temper about to boil over.

Manish was one of our best men in India, our eyes and ears back home. He had gone M.I.A. last night while we were at the club. I had been on my way up to the suite to call my guys in private when I had found Amelia cornered by some fucker. She had distracted me.

"Abandoned train car in Bengal. His body was mangled. Missing fingers and toes. Slash wounds to the gut and throat. They say he bled out," Jai responded somberly.

"Do we have a location on Tarun yet?" He was an expert at hiding and had been doing it for most of his adult life. We had planted men all over India, especially in Bengal, to find him. Unfortunately, none of them had been successful yet. Even with our best tracking software, we could not find a location.

"Once the tracking app from IP Innovations is complete, we may be able to locate him," Jai offered. He was a tech genius, so I trusted his confidence.

The real reason we bought startups was so that we could keep tabs on all the players in our world, especially Tarun. We were able to gather various bits of data from different apps we acquired to put together full profiles of each person in our drug network, like a web of data of the underground.

Tarun's profile had been more than difficult to compile. We were only able to find information from his teen years, when the internet first started collecting data from users. The most updated photo we had of him was from when he was eighteen years old. That was also the last time any of us had seen him in person. None of the information we found was helpful, since it was now outdated. He had been able to raise a tech team of his own to block the retrieval of his own data and cloak his photos so he couldn't be tracked. He was elusive from photographs. He remained hidden away from anyone except his closest men to avoid recognition. To the rest of the world, he was still a fat kid with a double chin and a large, dark-brown birthmark on the left side of his neck. We hoped that with the app from IP Innovations, we could track him using their feature that altered images to find a hit. Amelia was oblivious to how useful she was to us by having created this feature.

To the outside world, Sethi Tech just seemed like another tech giant who bought over startups with innovative apps. However, the only apps we were interested in were tracking apps. Sure, we acquired some random non-tracking apps from other startups too, but that was just to throw off the public.

Tarun knew what we were up to and was trying desperately to block our advances. He was most likely unaware that he couldn't trick the new software we had acquired. I had ordered Jason to push his developers to implement the feature and had him sign an NDA so he could not discuss it with anyone. We had made his staff do the same. They had assumed it was just regular paperwork that needed to be signed in an acquisition. All we needed now was a current photo of Tarun without any prosthetics or physical alterations to his face and a location of where the photo had been taken.

"His network in the States is still growing," Jai said before he took another puff from his cigar.

This guy had some balls to think he could spy on us and then take our business. He had already lost his brother. Was he stupid enough to continue his dream of a takeover?

"Not for long." His little fantasy did not stand a chance.

VIII. Amelia

The next week was a blur. All the developers were in a rush to complete our features. We were working on no sleep and copious amounts of coffee. Everyone wanted to do a good job to avoid being laid off.

However, I still had mixed feelings about possibly working for Sethi Tech. On one hand, I knew that something shady was going on in that company and that Shyam was responsible for it. My intuition told me that the rumors were true. But at the same time, I couldn't stop myself from thinking of him. I secretly hoped he would visit the office again before we delivered our product, just so I could see him again. I also hated him for leaving me hanging *twice*, yet I couldn't deny how he made me feel. My body always betrayed my brain when I was around him. It kept asking for more.

Friday came and no one had heard word about moving over to Sethi Tech. We felt defeated, even though we had miraculously completed our product on time.

Jason didn't have an update for us either. He thanked us for our hard work and wished us luck in our "future endeavors." I guess he didn't care as much, since he was getting a huge payout for *his* software. He'd probably just create another startup like all the other startup CEOs and make even more money selling that one too.

When five o'clock came around, Nat and I said our goodbyes. We hugged and kissed each other as the reality of not working together anymore sank in. I was going to miss her. We promised to meet up for lunch soon so we could sulk about being laid off. I also bid farewell to the rest of my coworkers. The mood was somber as we all left the office for the last time.

It was raining when I left the building. How appropriate. It matched my mood—dreary and dismal. I could have called a cab, but instead, I chose to walk in the rain and just let myself feel my emotions.

This was my first job out of college. I had never been laid off before, so this type of rejection was new. I knew I was smart and felt confident when it came to my work, but this layoff had bruised my ego.

I reached my apartment door and inserted my key into the lock. The door pushed open before I even had the chance to turn the key. *Huh?* I thought I had locked my door when I left this morning. I looked around before entering. My place was so small that it was easy to scan without stepping inside. Nothing seemed out of place. And I had my most valuable item with me, my laptop.

I quietly stepped inside and slid off my soaked shoes so they wouldn't squeak on the floor. Tiptoeing further into my apartment, I checked the closet and the bathroom. No one seemed to be hiding in there. I was being paranoid. I must have left the door unlocked by accident. It made sense, since my mind had been preoccupied lately.

I took a long, hot shower and changed into some pajamas for comfort. It had been a while since I had called my mom. She had lived alone since my dad passed and I moved to the city. Luckily, she still worked as a nurse, so she had something to keep her busy and distracted from the loneliness.

I plopped onto my bed and dialed her number.

"Hi, sweetie! I was just thinking about you!" Her voice always sounded bright and happy whenever I called home. It broke my heart even more that I had left her alone.

"Hi, Mom," I said, pretending everything was okay.

"What's wrong, dear?" I could never hide my mood from her. We were so close that we could always sense when the other was upset.

"I think I just got laid off from work. I guess I feel disappointed."

"Are you sure?" she asked. I filled her in on the takeover and how none of us had heard any word about being rolled over to the new company.

"Amelia, you're a smart girl. Feel what you need to feel right now, but then move on. Tonight, you can allow yourself to sulk, but tomorrow, start looking for something new." She always pushed me to be strong. After my dad died, she realized how much she had relied on her husband. She was lost for a while and struggled to manage the household bills, since my dad had done everything. She didn't want me to ever be in

47

that position, so she always pushed me to be independent.

"You're right, Mom," I said with resolve. "I'll start searching tomorrow." I would find something even better than my last job and start a new chapter in my career.

"That's my girl. You'll find something fast. I just know it. You're too brilliant not to." Her voice was full of motherly pride.

"Thanks. So, what's new with you?" I asked.

"Well, work is busy since it's flu season. A lot of people are being admitted into the hospital." Her voice sounded tired when she spoke of work. I wished she could retire, and I could support her financially. Maybe my next job would allow me to do so eventually.

"That's rough. Be careful, mom. I wouldn't want you to catch anything either." She worked in the emergency department, so she was first in line to catch whatever infectious disease wandered in.

She laughed. "Don't worry, dear. That's *my* job."

I sighed, suddenly feeling exhausted from the emotions of the day. "I miss you, Mom. I think I'm going to sleep now. I love you." I hadn't slept properly in forever because I had been working so much. Tonight, I would not work on code. I needed a mental break.

"I love you, too. You know you can always come back home to visit whenever you need to, right?"

A vacation sounded amazing, but I really did need to figure out my job situation before planning a trip.

"I do," I replied. "Thanks, Mom. Bye."

"Goodbye, sweetie," she said before hanging up.

I lay back on my pillows and closed my eyes allowing sleep to take over my body.

****

The next day, I took my mom's advice and started my job search. I had slept all evening and into the morning, and woke up feeling rejuvenated.

I was determined to find something even better than IP Innovations. I polished up my resumé and updated my LinkedIn profile. I found a few positions and submitted applications to be considered. I was excited about finding a new job. A fresh start.

I was about to take a break and make myself a sandwich when my phone buzzed with a text. I stared at the message in confusion.

Ms. Becker, please plan to arrive at Sethi Tech at 8 a.m. on Monday morning. Show your identification to security at the lobby to check in. – S. Sethi

IX. Amelia

Sethi Tech was located in one of the most beautiful pieces of architecture in the city. Panels of glass with steel supports towered high into the sky. So chic and modern. I was in awe as I stepped through the large glass doors.

The heels of my black ankle boots tapped against the black onyx floor of the lobby. I approached the front desk. The security guard asked for my identification as he made a phone call. I assumed he was letting someone know that I was checking in. As he hung up, he handed me a visitor's badge, which I clipped to the lapel of my blazer. The guard inspected the inside of my laptop bag and its contents before he motioned for me to wait in the large seating area off to the side.

I took a seat on one of the gray leather couches and placed my bag next to me. I watched the men and women who entered the lobby. They were all dressed impeccably, despite working for a tech company. The industry was known for its casual work attire; programmers usually wore jeans and t-shirts to work. The college-student vibe was alive and well in my world. Employers valued performance over appearance. Some of our most brilliant minds were dressed in beat-up tennis shoes and hoodies.

Watching the parade of well-dressed people made me aware of how underdressed I was, though in my mind, I *had* dressed up this morning, wearing a burgundy corduroy blazer with a white blouse over black denim leggings and black leather ankle boots. I had even taken a little extra time on my hair and straightened it. My makeup was minimal: pink lip gloss, nude eyeshadow, and a little mascara for a clean and fresh look. I told myself that I had put the extra effort into my appearance because I wanted to make a good first impression, but inside, I knew that I'd most likely run into Shyam, and it was possible I was attempting to make him regret rejecting me. It was petty, but I was still bitter about him leaving me.

When I had gotten his text, I had been angry at how distant his tone sounded—impersonal and cold masked as "professional." I mean, the man had had his hands down my pants, so I would have thought we were beyond formalities.

I had been about to send a reply of "screw you," but reconsidered when I'd eyed the resumé on my monitor. It was short. Too short. I had a lot of accomplishments in college, but my post-college section was bare. It only included my job at IP Innovations. It would be difficult to find a better job with just months of experience at a startup. Under normal circumstances, I wouldn't even have been considered for a job at a tech giant like Sethi Tech with my limited experience. But here the opportunity was staring me in the face, and I had been about to turn it down.

The industry wasn't particularly welcoming to women as it was. It was an uphill battle to be taken seriously in interviews by the older men who ran these companies. The industry was a game, and you had to play it smart if you were a woman. It couldn't hurt to see what Shyam had to offer me at Sethi Tech. Listing this job on my resumé would certainly jumpstart my career.

A tall woman dressed in a crisp white shirt and tight black pencil skirt that hit just below her knees stood in front of the waiting area. "Amelia Becker?" she called out as she glanced at my badge.

"That's me," I replied and stood up, bag in hand.

"Nice to meet you, Ms. Becker." She extended her perfectly manicured hand to me. "I'm Jessica, head of Human Resources, and I will be conducting your orientation today."

I shook her hand. "Nice to meet you, too."

"Please, follow me and we'll get started." She released my hand and spun around on her four-inch black pumps. She walked with such poise and grace as she led me to a set of elevators. She was a model, and the world was her catwalk.

She tapped her badge to a chip reader on a panel adjacent to the doors. The elevator dinged before the doors opened. I followed Jessica inside and eyed the buttons for the floor numbers. Thirty-eight floors! I was used to working in a single-floor office with shared tables for workspaces.

Jessica pressed the button for floor twenty-five and the doors closed.

I was amazed as I peered out at the view outside of the glass elevator as we ascended. How did one ever get used to working in such a grand building?

"You'll find that today will mostly be filled with housekeeping tasks. Orientation usually involves filling out paperwork, completing harassment training, and working with the IT department to set up your computer," Jessica said as the elevator rose to our destination.

"I brought my own laptop, so I can work from that if it would be easier," I offered.

"I am afraid we do not allow external laptops to be used, for security purposes. You will be given a computer that works on a higher bandwidth to customize to your liking."

"Oh, okay," I replied. At least my new computer would be faster than my laptop.

The elevator came to a smooth stop and the doors opened. "This is us," Jessica announced as she exited with me in tow.

X. Amelia

After hours of paperwork and training modules on one of the HR computers, I was ready to set up my own computer.

Jessica led me to the elevators again. This time, she pressed the button for thirty-eight as I entered behind her. *The top floor?* I had assumed I'd be working on one of the lower levels. Surely, the top level was reserved for important people like board members, not a new programmer. If I was going to be working on the top floor, then that meant I'd run into...

My heart was racing as the elevator halted and the doors opened to reveal a tall and tanned figure with gorgeous black hair. He had been looking down at his phone before he heard the elevator ding, announcing itself. *Jai.*

I let out a sigh of relief. I'd had little interaction with this Sethi brother, but I couldn't have been more glad to see him. I wasn't ready to face his sibling just yet.

"Good afternoon, Mr. Sethi," Jessica greeted him in a most professional manner.

"Hey, Jessica," he replied casually, flashing her a bright smile. Jai was handsome, just like his brother. They looked so similar, with beautifully golden skin and dark features, except Jai had dark-brown eyes—like coffee. His boyish charm led me to believe that he was the younger brother. Shyam always looked serious and pensive, just like an oldest child. Jai was more jovial, which made me feel more at ease standing in front of him. It also helped that he was dressed more casually than any of the other people in the building—in a pair of jeans and a fitted white t-shirt that clung to his muscular torso.

He eyed me as Jessica made the introductions. "Mr. Sethi, may I introduce to you Amelia Becker, formerly of IP Innovations? Ms. Becker, this is Mr. Sethi." She redirected her attention to Jai. "I was just showing Ms. Becker to her new workspace."

Jai hesitated as he considered what Jessica had just said. His eyebrow raised after a couple of seconds as he seemed to reach his conclusion. His lips spread into a sly smile.

"Of course. Hello, Amelia." He offered me his hand. "I hope Jessica hasn't been boring you with all that HR red tape." His voice carried a similar Indian-mixed-with-British accent to Shyam's, but it was less pronounced. I could also hear a little more of an American accent come through, unlike when Shyam spoke.

"Not at all," I answered quickly, noticing Jessica shift uncomfortably next to me. HR wasn't exactly exciting, but that wasn't her fault.

"Well, come on. I'll show you the fun part of the tour," he said as he motioned for me to follow him. "I'll take it from here, Jessica."

"She is in thirty-eight F," Jessica offered and stayed behind as Jai showed me the way.

The entire building was impeccably designed, but the thirty-eighth floor was beyond magnificent. There was a large fountain in the entrance way, right in front of the elevators. The fountain flowed into a large infinity pond filled with water plants and koi fish leisurely swimming around. It was an extravagant sight, but it fit with the modern style of the building.

Sensing my astonishment, Jai joked, "I know. Not a bad place to go to work, huh?"

"Not at all. This place is beautiful," I replied in awe.

"We hired the city's best architect to be able to structure a koi pond on the top floor. Trust me, it was no easy feat."

We continued along the perimeter of the pond, passing a set of large glass doors that opened to a large room with a shiny conference table and several leather office chairs inside.

Jai pointed to the doors. "On the right is one of our conference rooms. We have two on this floor. The other is on the opposite side."

The conference room seemed much bigger and more lavish than the conference room at IP Innovations, from what I could see through the glass windows. I blushed, remembering the old conference room and what Shyam had done to me in there.

"Now, *this* is my favorite part." Jai made a sharp right and led me down a shorter hallway. We entered what looked like an industrial kitchen. There were cooking stations set at several kitchen islands, each with its own chef working efficiently over the flames.

"You can order almost any meal you'd like to eat from one of our chefs, and they will prepare everything for you in-house." Jai wandered over to one of the chefs and patted him on the back as he worked diligently.

"Wow! This is so impressive! I pretty much just ate at the food trucks next to my old job every day for lunch." Even though I loved tacos, it wasn't as good as having a private chef at work.

"Hey, now, food trucks aren't half-bad. I like that new taco truck that moved in there a few weeks ago," Jai said as he walked to one of the deluxe espresso machines and drew himself a shot in a small cup. "Want one?" he offered.

I declined. "I don't take you as a food truck aficionado," I teased.

"Hey, don't judge. They are life savers at two in the morning when you're wasted and starving."

I giggled at his response. I couldn't imagine a rich and powerful Sethi brother coming down with the munchies.

"But seriously. Feel free to order anything you want to your office. Here, catch!" He tossed me a snack bag, and I caught a glimpse of silver on his finger. It looked just like the ring Shyam wore.

"Gummy bears?" I asked, examining the bag in my hands. "Who orders gummy bears on *this* floor?" I chuckled. I couldn't imagine any of the "suits" indulging in gummy snacks.

"The chefs are always prepared for any request. You'd be surprised at what you'll find in here if you raid the pantry." Jai placed his empty espresso cup in one of the sinks and led me back into the common area.

With my gummy bears in hand, we stopped at another glass door. *38-F Amelia Becker.* I opened my eyes wider to read it again, in case my eyes were playing tricks on me.

"Welcome to your new office," Jai announced as he opened the doors and strolled inside.

My feet barely responded enough to bring me past the threshold. A gorgeous white desk with platinum legs stood at the far end. On top of the desktop were white and platinum accessories that matched each other perfectly.

Opposite the desk was a seating area with a dark-blue velvet sofa and a sleek glass coffee table. Two matching armchairs sat across from the sofa. It looked like a living room featured in an architectural magazine.

The far wall of the office was made up of tall windows. I stepped closer to them to peer at the view of the city. I could see yellow cabs zooming down the street and people hustling to get to where they needed to be.

"This must be a mistake," I managed to say. This had to be a dream. "Are you sure I'm supposed to be in here?"

"Your name is on the door, isn't it?" Jai replied coolly. He leaned against the wall, looking like a model with his hands in his pockets and one leg crossed over the other. "Let's get IT on the phone and get your desktop set up, shall we?"

"Um, sure." I wasn't ready to stop staring out of the windows, but I gave in as I followed him to my new desk.

XI. Shyam

Work had been a shit show from the moment I stepped foot into the office this morning. The most recent data-tracking reports showed that Tarun's network was growing rapidly on the West Coast and in the Midwest. We still had an extensive stronghold on the East Coast, but map data implied that his network was closing in on us at an alarming rate.

I had spent an hour on the phone with one of my men, going over logistics for our next product shipment to Spain. Saran had assured me that we were on track to finish production within in the next week and then ship directly from our port in Staten Island.

Since we were officially known as a tech company, we often shipped computer parts that we produced cheaply to hide our product in the cargo. This time, we planned to send ten crates of central processing units and monitors to conceal our product. We needed this shipment to be received without error if we wanted to break even.

With all the issues needing my attention, I had not been able to see Amelia yet. Security had alerted me of her arrival, but I had been tied up. I knew that Jessica had kept her busy all morning with orientation procedures. I looked at the clock—right about now, she should be with the IT department, setting up her computer. Just thinking about her stirred a desire to seek her out. To check on her. To touch her.

My need won out. Leaving my suit jacket hanging on the back of my chair, I pushed back from my desk and wandered out of the office to find my new employee.

As I approached her door, I heard a feminine laugh, followed by a deep male voice. I pushed my way in without knocking to announce myself.

Amelia was seated in front of her computer, while Jai hovered behind her with his elbow resting on the back of her chair. They were both looking at something on her monitor. Her face looked bright and relaxed as she looked up at Jai while he pointed to her screen. I had never seen her look so at ease. Every time she was around me, she seemed tense—even scared. Anger bubbled inside of me that Jai was experiencing a side of her that I had yet to see.

I slammed the door closed behind me, shaking the walls as the door hit the frame. Amelia and Jai turned their heads abruptly in my direction. The smile on her face quickly faded when she realized where the noise had come from.

"Hey, man. You found us." Jai stayed hunched over her chair as he smirked at me. I didn't appreciate his proximity to her, or the stupid cocky expression on his face.

"Why are you in here?" My voice was tight with anger I had failed to suppress.

"Just helping Amelia here get settled into her new office." Jai lowered his gaze to her and gave her a wink.

She smiled awkwardly back at him, unsure of how to react with the tension in the room.

My blood was boiling. Jai was a flirt by nature, which didn't bother me. However, I didn't like that Amelia was now the subject of his flirtation.

"Don't we have an IT department to do that?" I barked.

"Why bother them when she could have the Chief Technical Officer of the company help her set up her hardware? Gotta make the new hires feel welcomed, you know," he jested.

"Leave," I growled.

Amelia clasped her hands in her lap and shifted uncomfortably in her chair.

Jai raised both of his hands in front of his chest in surrender.

As he passed by me on his way out, he lowered his voice so only I could hear him. "So, now we're keeping employees a secret?"

I didn't have a response. How could I answer him when I wasn't even sure why I had brought her on? I had told myself it was because she was a good developer. But was there another reason?

Just after he walked out of the door, Jai stuck his head back in and flashed his biggest smile at Amelia to tease me even more. "If you need any more IT help, you know where to find me." The door clicked behind him.

Amelia rose from her chair and stood facing me from behind her desk. "Shyam...I mean, Mr. Sethi. I'm sorry for taking up so much of Jai...um, Mr. Sethi's time," she stammered.

I liked seeing her nervous around me—seeing the effect I had on her.

I stalked closer to her, as if I were a predator closing in on my prey. "I trust you are ready to work now. You and Jai have wasted enough time for one day. The next time you need help with setup, contact our IT department instead." I couldn't hold back my aggression.

She stared at me with a look of disbelief. "He was just helping!" she snapped as her hands balled into tight fists at her sides.

My eyebrow arched with curiosity. *This kitten has claws.* Hearing her raised voice was another first for me. Clearly, she had some fight in her. She just needed to be pushed.

"Talking back to your boss? And on your first day? Not a great way to make a good first impression." I continued moving in until I was near enough to feel her forceful exhalations of anger on my skin. Her frustration spurred me on even more.

"Only when I think he's being unfair," she shot back. Her attitude surprised me, yet it made my dick hard. I wanted her to obey me and fall in line, but her fight made me horny as hell.

She had to tilt her head back to show me the venom in her eyes because I was so much taller than her. A lock of her thick hair had fallen over her face during her tantrum, and it blew back and forth with each breath that huffed from her nose. I lifted it gently with my fingertips, feeling its smoothness. I tucked it behind her ear and let my finger slide along her cheek, which was warm with anger.

I studied the beautiful face before me. Her glossed lips were full, just waiting for me to sink my teeth into them. Her breath slowed to almost a complete stop as I lifted her chin and moved my face closer to hers. My fingers slid to her neck. Her bruises had disappeared, but I still remembered them vividly, along with the asshole who had given them to her. I stroked her neck gently, silently apologizing on behalf of her attacker.

Her hands moved to my forearms as if to tell me, *Don't stop.* I did not want to stop, either. Her hold over me was inexplicable. I had never felt the need to be in control and yet be so out of control at the same time before. *What is she doing to me?*

Her delicate hands slid from my arms to my chest. *Can she feel my heart beating faster?*

Rising onto her toes, she closed the gap between us. She took control. *My control.* Her plump lips pressed against mine. Her kiss was gentle, as if to test my desire. I needed to taste her. I needed to consume her with my mouth.

I ran my tongue along the seam of her lips, seeking an invitation. Ever so responsive, she invited me in. Our tongues met with fervor. She tasted like strawberries. The heat between us was so strong.

Gripping my shirt with her fingers, she pressed her body against my hard length. I sucked her bottom lip between my teeth and bit down hard. She breathed out a pleasured moan, bringing me back to my senses.

I released her lip and stared into those dark-green eyes. *Fuck*. I needed to get a hold of myself.

Just then, a knock sounded at the door.

XII. Amelia

My body was buzzing from our kiss as Shyam's eyes, hooded with desire, stared into mine—mirroring my need. I had been upset that he rejected me before and had even wondered if I was the only one who felt the attraction. But in this moment, I knew he felt it too.

He had stormed into the office and forced Jai out when he was just helping me get settled, and then he had ordered me around like a child until I couldn't take it anymore. He had pushed me, and I had snapped—but not enough to resist the spark between us. The man could kiss. It was the best kiss I had ever had, and I would never forget it.

A knock at the door pulled him out of our trance. Stepping back from me, he smoothed the front of his shirt and wiped the remnants of my lip gloss from his lips with his fingers.

Anxiety shot through my body at the idea of being caught in a compromising position on my first day. I already felt out of place in this luxurious building. Getting caught making out with the boss would only make things more awkward.

"Come in," Shyam commanded in his usual authoritative tone, but his voice was laced with irritation.

The door cracked open and Jessica stepped inside. "Oh, Mr. Sethi." She glanced nervously between Shyam and me, probably unsure of what to make of her boss being in my office. Whatever she was thinking, she didn't expose it. She maintained her professional manner. "I'm sorry to interrupt."

"Do you need something?" Shyam asked, not bothering to disguise his impatience.

Sensing his mood, Jessica answered hurriedly, "I just received Ms. Becker's keycard and I wanted to deliver it as soon as possible."

She held out a small card with my name and photo on it. I looked like I was twelve years old in the photo I had taken only hours earlier. I always looked much younger than my age. And standing next to a confident man like Shyam while I was still flushed from our make-out session probably made me look like jailbait right now.

"Thank you," I said as I took the card from her. "And, please, call me Amelia."

Jessica looked to Shyam, uncertain of how to respond. He glared back. His annoyance at how long this conversation had already carried on was obvious.

"You're welcome, Amelia," she said, visibly uncomfortable with this level of informality. "You can wear this one instead of the guest badge that you have right now. It controls access to the elevators and labs."

"Labs?" I asked. *Why would anyone need to use a computer lab when they had a huge private office to work from?* I already knew I would be more productive in my new office than I had been at my tiny desk at IP Innovations.

"Thank you, Jessica," Shyam cut her off before she could respond. "That will be all."

Jessica must have been used to his curtness because she didn't flinch. "Yes, sir," she said and exited the office, leaving us alone once again.

Shyam directed his attention to me again as he tucked both hands into his pants pockets.

Searching for something to say to break the tension, I dropped my gaze to my hands. *The keycard.* "Do you really have computer labs here?"

A slow, mischievous smile spread to his lips. God, he was even more handsome when he smiled, even if it was devious in nature. *How is that possible?*

"Now that we've had our playtime, let's get to work. Come with me." He held the door open for me, allowing me to walk ahead of him.

He put his hands in his pockets again as we walked in silence down the hall. He obviously wasn't much of a talker. It worked for me because I was generally shy with strangers. *Is he a stranger, though?* I had just tasted him with my tongue and felt his length against my body.

We walked past the bank of elevators that Jessica and I had used earlier, arriving instead at another elevator bank with only one elevator. Shyam scanned his keycard on the scanner and ushered me inside. My intuition told me to turn and run away. But I didn't listen.

Inside the elevator, there was only one button, marked with a "B." *B for Basement?* This elevator had only one destination—deep down under this world of well-dressed employees and marble floors. Once I descended, would I ever return?

He pressed the button and stepped back in line with me in the elevator car. As if knowing my trepidation, Shyam eyed me silently from his periphery as we descended. Maybe he felt guilty for plunging me into whatever darkness I was about to experience. Or maybe he didn't feel any guilt at all. Maybe he enjoyed pulling me under with him.

The doors opened, and this time, Shyam exited first. He forwent all manners he had shown me previously in the world above and guided me into this world.

The "basement" looked nothing like the rest of the building. It was unpolished and bare. Paint chipped off the walls, and the floors were made of unfinished cement. A long hallway extended from the elevator, with no doors or windows in sight. There was no natural light like there had been on the top floor of the building. No floor-to-ceiling windows with expensive light fixtures. Instead, bare bulbs hung from the ceiling in between exposed pipes.

Shyam was already midway down the hall when he turned and noticed I wasn't following him. My brain was screaming at me to turn around and never come back.

Whatever was down here wasn't something that I should involve myself with. Instead, I swallowed the lump in my throat and walked slowly toward my guide for protection. I couldn't explain the safety I felt when I was close to him, especially when he was most likely the devil, and this was probably his playground.

We walked to the end of the stark hallway and turned a quick left, stopping at a door just past the corner. There were no windows around it, so I couldn't tell what was inside. There was a scanner beside the door, but it was much higher than the others I had seen in the rest of the building, and a lot bigger. Shyam took my hand and pulled me closer to him, then lifted my hair and pulled it back from my face. The back of my neck tickled in anticipation as he moved behind me, holding my hair firmly in one hand. I was sure he could see the goosebumps that spread over my skin. He gently pushed my chin forward with his other hand until my eyes were in front of the device. I rose on my tip-toes to reach it better. *A retina scanner.*

This must have been why I'd had to take an eye exam during my HR orientation. I had been told that they were just taking photos of my eyes to test for vision problems. It had seemed weird, but I'd figured these big companies were just extra careful when it came to workplace liabilities. In actuality, they had scanned my retina for access to the labs. I felt stupid for not questioning it more at the time.

The scanner beeped in approval and a click sounded. Shyam opened the door and stepped through, with me behind him.

Motion-sensing lights flicked on as we entered the room. Three rows of computers, each with dual screens, filled the entirely white room. No one else was inside but us. It surely *was* a computer lab. *But why does it need to be in a basement so far from employee use? And why is no one else using it?*

Shyam pulled out a chair in front of one of the computer stations and motioned for me to sit. He hovered behind me and lifted my index finger to a fingerprint scanner next to the keyboard. *Why all these security measures?* Suddenly, the left monitor lit up with a white outline of the world map. Little white dots freckled the map and moved jerkily, like video-game characters on the move. The right monitor projected tables of data—data linked to each one of the moving dots. It was biographic data about people. They were tracking people!

Astonished, I stared at the moving dots while the tables of data updated automatically. "What is this?" I whispered, unsure of who I was talking to—Shyam or myself.

"Tracking data for anyone of interest to my company," he answered my hanging question.

"Like owners of new startups?" I asked, hoping the answer would be something benign, even though I knew better. It was common for tech companies to collect private data from users, but what they did with that information was another story.

"Anyone who is involved with buying our product," he corrected.

He read the confusion that was etched onto my face and continued, "Drugs, Amelia *jaan."* Dear.

My heart slammed against my chest. The rumors were true. Shyam and Jai really were drug dealers. And this data was being used for something bad. Very bad.

"Is this why you bought IP Innovations? For our tracking software?" It was all starting to make sense to me.

"Yes," he answered bluntly.

I swallowed hard against the bile in my throat. "Why do you need me if you already have the software?"

"I am using it to find information about a specific person." He had answered all my questions so far, but I got the sense he was holding back, only offering answers to what I asked. Nothing more.

Don't ask. Curiosity got the best of me. "Who?"

"I will never lie to you when you ask me a question, so be careful of the things you wish to know." His warning lingered over me like a dark cloud cautioning of a tumultuous storm. "Do you still want to know?"

Did I? Could I still get out of the underworld? I didn't have to know his answer. I signed an NDA during the acquisition and legally couldn't discuss anything I knew about the software, including this, with anyone. I could go back home to Seattle and pretend none of this had ever happened.

When I didn't respond, he continued, "A competitor and my biggest enemy."

"Another drug dealer?" I already knew what he was going to say.

"Yes."

Dread filled my gut. "Why do you need information on him?"

"He betrayed an alliance set by our families generations ago. There are boundaries in this business, and he disobeyed them."

"Where does he live?" I couldn't stop myself from finding out more.

"India. I don't have an exact location yet. His base is in Bengal, but he has been in hiding." Shyam sighed, letting out some of the frustration he seemed to be holding in.

"And you need the tracking software to find him?" Our software would be useful for tracking down someone of color.

"He is the only person in this network that I do not have useful data on." He tensed up, clenching his jaw.

"Why?" I found that perplexing. It was rare that anyone could evade tracking software. Every app collected some sort of data on a user. The only way someone could avoid having their data collected was for them to essentially live off the grid and not engage in any modern technology. No cellphone. No computers. No credit cards.

"He has an IT team of his own to block any tracking software we've implemented to collect data on him. It's almost like he doesn't exist."

"And if you had facial-recognition software that was unaffected by cloaking, then you could accurately track him?" I was finally understanding Shyam's need for our software, and why he needed it so quickly.

He stroked a finger along the side of my cheek. I closed my eyes, savoring the contact, drunk off his touch. "The software your team created would fill the void that my current software has. By combining the two, I can locate him. You have working knowledge of the facial-recognition component, and I need you to use your anti-cloaking feature to find Tarun."

His name is Tarun? Knowing the name of Shyam's adversary made it even more personal.

"Jessica mentioned this lab. Do all of your employees know it exists?" I couldn't imagine why he'd let other people know about this lab or what his "night job" was.

"We do have other labs in the building used strictly for Sethi Tech development—that is, what our employees *think* Sethi Tech development is. Our employees have no idea about our drugs and our network. This lab is only used by Jai, our men who aid us in moving our product, and myself. Only a select handful of people know of it or have access to it. Jessica doesn't know what it is used for. As for the location, the lab is most secure in the basement, where hackers are unable to fish for our internet signal and break into our system. We can work in privacy down here without worrying about prying eyes, both in the real world and the virtual world."

"What will you do when you find him?" I regretted asking as soon as the words flew out of my mouth. He was a criminal. I didn't have to be one to know how they treated their enemies.

He stood up straight behind me. The loss of his warmth was almost painful; up until now, it had kept me steady and grounded. "I think that's a question that you don't really want answered," he said.

I changed my line of questioning, afraid of what he might say if I pressed him. I turned my face to look up at him. "What if I don't want to help you?"

His hazel eyes fixed on mine. "Then you can sever all ties with Sethi Tech."

I can leave? That would mean I would have to cut ties with Shyam too. "How do you know I won't report you to the police?"

"You signed an NDA. Legally, you cannot discuss the software, or anything you have seen or heard at Sethi Tech, with anyone. And the police would never dare get in our way."

Of course, he had the cops in his pocket. He owned the biggest tech company in America. He had enough money to buy the entire police force if he wanted to.

"Why can't you just have Jai do all of this?" Jai was a tech genius and his most trusted confidant, since he was blood, so it would be more fitting for his brother to tailor the facial-recognition software.

"He's a brilliant programmer like you, but he didn't build this program. You did." I blushed at his compliment. One minute, he was telling me he was an international drug dealer, and in the next, he was making me feel like a blushing schoolgirl.

"Are you prepared to help me?" His eyes were dark and intense.

I still had so many questions. My mind was racing, and I was no longer capable of putting together coherent streams of thought. I couldn't decide right now. Logically, I should leave this company and run far from this man. But a pit formed in my stomach at the thought of never seeing him again.

I exhaled before responding. "I need time."

XIII. Amelia

After Shyam's revelation in the lab, I desired space to think. Shyam didn't say much after I told him I couldn't decide immediately, though he seemed withdrawn. The wall that had slowly been crumbling, brick by brick every time we were together, was fully erected again. He said I could take the rest of the week off and give him my answer by the weekend—spoken like a true boss and not someone who was attracted to me.

I spent my time off mindlessly coding for random projects that I had started in the past but never had a chance to finish because I was always busy with work. Every so often, Shyam's face would burn my mind as I coded. I could feel his commanding touch on my skin. I could taste his lips on mine. In the short time that I had known him, he had gained total control of my body in a way I hadn't known a man could. We hadn't even had sex yet, but I felt like he knew me so intimately. My heart felt heavy every time I thought about walking away from this beautifully intense man.

I should quit. I knew it was the right decision. But it felt wrong to consider it. I was green in my career, but I knew I could pave my way in this world of men if given the chance. I just needed to play my cards right.

I thought working for Sethi Tech would fast-track my path to becoming a Senior Developer. But how could I be an honest programmer while working for a company that ultimately made dirty money? What if I got caught by authorities for my role at Sethi Tech? I would become a casualty and land myself in federal prison for aiding drug dealers. Plus, the government wasn't too keen on civilians using facial-recognition software for tracking people down. I knew Shyam had said he controlled the police, but little people like me were usually thrown to the wolves to protect the guys running the operation. I really didn't know him that well. How could I trust that he wouldn't turn me in to save his skin if he ever needed to? A part of me knew that I could trust him, but how could I be completely certain?

I was a logical person by nature. It was how a developer's brain worked. My thoughts were usually based in "cause and effect"—if I participated in illegal acts, then I would probably get arrested. If I stayed at Sethi Tech, and didn't get caught by the police, I could move up in the tech world.

This was the first time my emotions had gotten in the way of making a decision. I wasn't used to this feeling, having my heart rule my head. It was stupid. We weren't even in a relationship. I shouldn't base my decision on something uncertain.

All these thoughts did nothing to alleviate the ache I felt when I thought about handing in my resignation and leaving Shyam for good. I wanted to see more of him. I wanted to feel him. He was the only man who could turn me on just by being in the same room. I had never felt this attraction with another man before Shyam.

My phone buzzed, pulling me out of the dizzying spiral of thoughts that had sucked me under.

Hey, hotshot! Remember me?! Come out with me tonight! Unless you're too busy with your fancy new job!

Natalie. I had forgotten that we had talked about meeting up. I had never gotten back to her to set a date, but I didn't feel like going out tonight.

I'm so sorry! I completely forgot to text back. Actually, I'm not feeling up to going out. Probably just going to call it an early night.

My phone lit up with a call. *Shit.* She was persistent.

I answered, knowing she was calling to harass me. "Hey."

"Don't 'hey' me, you bore. First, you don't text me back, and then you try to weasel out of going out with me?" she demanded in her larger-than-life voice. I missed her personality in my life.

"I just feel like staying in tonight. It's been a long week." *Too long.*

"Mel, what's wrong?" she asked. "You sound depressed."

"Just stuff with the new job." I didn't want to get into details over the phone.

"Uh-oh. Those Sethi brothers treating you like shit? Do I need to show up at that office and straighten them out?" Natalie and I weren't related, but she always treated me like her little sister. It was a nice feeling, since I didn't have any siblings of my own.

79

I debated how much I should share with her. I definitely wouldn't tell her about the drug-dealing stuff, but I could share the hooking-up part. Shyam wasn't her boss, so it was okay to confide in her, right? Plus, this stuff was just festering inside me. It would be helpful to vent. "Um, not really. Well, just one brother, I suppose."

"Let me guess. The one who had eyes for you at Nirvana?"

She had noticed and never even harassed me about it? "Maybe. How did you know?"

"Are you serious? That man looked like he was ready to throw you down on a table and fuck you in front of the entire club." The image made me squeeze my thighs together to alleviate the ache.

"Hello? Earth to Mel?" *Oops.* I must have taken too long to respond while envisioning Shyam on top of me.

"Hmmm, yeah, I'm here." It was clear through my voice that I was distracted.

"OMG, you fucked him already?! And you didn't tell me?" She was practically yelling at me over the phone.

"What? No! I mean...Not really." *Just made out with lots of tongue and humped. Oh yeah, and finger-fucking.*

"Not really? Yeah, your ass is coming to the bar with me. I need details, now! I'll stop by in an hour to pick you up."

I didn't want to go, but I supposed I could use some girl talk and alcohol right now. Drinking alone at home just sounded sad.

I gave in. "Okay, fine. You won again at wearing me down."

"I always do, babe! See you soon!" she said before hanging up.

****

"Oh my God!" Nat sat at the bar, wide-eyed with disbelief at my soap opera of a situation. I had spared her all the illegal details. It was safer for her if she were truly oblivious to Shyam's criminal dealings. I also hadn't shared my thoughts about leaving Sethi Tech, because she'd have pressed me for a reason for wanting to.

"I have to say that I'm impressed," she continued.

"Impressed?" I asked, confused.

"Of all the men out there, you land Shyam Sethi! He has a reputation for being a hard ass. You cracked his shell!" She pounded on the table with her fist.

"I didn't 'land' him. I don't even know what we are. One minute, he can't keep his hands off me, and the next minute, he seems cold and distant." I sighed.

I finished off my second old fashioned, the liquid warming my belly on its way down. Nat motioned for the bartender to refill our drinks. I really wasn't a drinker, but I had been sulking at home all week and needed to numb some of my worry. It worked—all that liquor and no dinner had quickly gone to my head and made me willing to unload the drama I had been keeping secret.

"Your boss obviously likes you, if he made out with you on your first day." Nat nudged my arm with her elbow before taking a large swig of her beer.

Hearing her say that made me feel cheap, like I was just a piece of ass that Shyam had hired to mess around with on the side. I knew he had said he needed my help to track Tarun, but I couldn't share that part with Nat. Still, I didn't want anyone thinking I was fucking, or technically not-fucking, the boss for a job.

Sensing my irritation, she grabbed my hand. "Babe, that's not what I meant. You're fucking smart and you deserve this chance in your career. He would have been a damn fool not to hire you. I just meant that it sounds like he feels the same way about you as you do about him. I saw how he looked at you at the club. There's something there."

I sighed loudly. "I just wish we could have an honest discussion about what we are. I get too nervous to ask. And he's not much of a talker, either."

"That's because he's too busy sticking his tongue down your throat," she teased.

I pretended to be appalled and pulled my hand away from hers to smack her arm. "Nat!" That part was kind of true, though. And it sure was a nice tongue to have down one's throat.

We both giggled, too tipsy to care about how loud we were.

"But seriously, Mel. Being a woman in tech is enough of a struggle. Play the game and use this to your advantage. He hired you because of your brains. It's so hard for girls like us to make it in this industry. Don't let this fling you have with him ruin your career. I don't know him personally, but men with power like him have a way of using women to get what they want. You have a great opportunity at Sethi Tech, and I'd hate to see it thrown away because he got bored and found another girl. Be careful. Only get involved if you're sure he feels the same way as you and he's willing to commit to being in a relationship."

Working for Shyam *was* a big opportunity in my career. I could pretty much have any job I wanted with Sethi Tech on my resumé. I couldn't let my attraction to him get in the way of what I had worked so hard for.

As for the criminal activities he was asking me to be a part of, I would need something worth a lot more than a great salary and benefits to do what he was asking of me. If the police were in his pocket, the likelihood of getting caught was low. However, I was more concerned with my moral standing.

Nat was right. This industry was a game, and I had to play it smart to make it big. I could put this job on my resumé and settle into an executive position at another tech giant on the West Coast, closer to home. I could financially support Mom so she could retire. I was willing to forego my morals if it meant I could take care of my mom for the rest of her life. The opportunity was staring right at me from a silver platter, and all I had to do was take it.

The bartender interrupted us with a new pair of drinks before I could respond to Nat.

"We didn't order these," I protested. My voice came out unsteady. It sounded different to my ears. The alcohol was definitely getting to me.

"They're on us." I froze and turned my head just enough to see two guys approaching us from behind.

"I'm Rob," said the tall one with perfectly styled blond hair as he perched on the stool next to Nat.

"And I'm Josh," said the shorter guy with sandy-brown hair.

"I'm Natalie, and this is Amelia," she said as she placed her hand into Rob's for a handshake that lasted longer than it should have. She was into this guy. I could tell from the way she batted her eyelashes and tucked her hair behind her ear after Rob released her hand.

I shook Josh's hand out of politeness. His grasp was cold and foreign to my skin. I quickly pulled my hand back.

"So, what are you ladies up to tonight?" Rob asked as he leaned in closer toward Nat.

"Not much. Just catching up with a little girl talk," Nat flirted back.

"I love when girls *talk,* especially in bed," Josh chimed in. *Jesus, he's cheesy.*

Sensing our girls' night was officially over, I was ready to go home. I had had too much to drink already and didn't want to sit around and make awkward small talk with horny guys. I stood up from my stool and threw some money onto the bar to close my tab. "Actually, I was just about to head home."

"How about I escort you, then?" Josh stood up too.

"Awww, Mel. Come on. Stay a little longer!" Nat pressed. Rob whispered something into her ear, and she giggled. They were soon lost in a conversation of their own.

"No, really. I'll be fine. I live nearby," I said hastily, hoping it would convince him not to follow me. I didn't like the idea of a stranger walking me home.

"It's okay. I don't mind. I'd love to get to know you better," Josh said as he placed his hand on the small of my back. I didn't like how it felt. It wasn't like when Shyam touched me. I only wanted his hands on me.

I stepped away from Josh's touch. "I need to use the restroom," I blurted out, then turned on my heel and walked quickly away.

In my periphery, I saw a couple of large and beefy men sitting at a table in the back of the room. They wore short-sleeved shirts and had tattoos covering the exposed skin on their arms and necks. This bar was usually frequented by millennials who worked at one of the office jobs around the area. These men looked out of place because they seemed a lot older and were dressed like bouncers at a club.

One of the men followed me with his gaze as I continued walking. I felt my heartrate speed up. Maybe I was just being paranoid because I was drunk. The alcohol was surely altering my mind.

I pulled my phone from my pocket and lowered my eyes to the screen to avoid his stare. I brought up the number I wanted to dial.

I stopped in front of the bathrooms and rested my back against the wall. My finger hovered over the phone icon on my screen. Inhaling a deep breath, I pressed it.

XIV. Shyam

I sat back in my chair with my scotch in hand. Jai sat across from me on a loveseat with a girl on his lap. She rolled her hips to the beat of the music. Her large tits were out, bouncing in his face as she moved and gyrated. Jai pulled the side of her G-string away and slipped a hundred-dollar bill close to her skin, then let go of the fabric, causing it to snap against her hip and eliciting an excited squeal from her. Our men scattered around the private suite chuckled, which invited more topless women to dance their way over to them.

Jai noticed my indifference. "What's up with you? Got somewhere else to be?" he said over the shoulder of his girl.

I ignored his smart-ass mouth and swirled the amber liquid in my glass. He liked to provoke me, just like any typical younger brother.

"Thinking about your redhead?" he kept jabbing.

"Don't you have your hands full right now?" I asked, nodding toward his hands gripping his girl's ass cheeks as she stroked her hips back and forth on his lap. "Shut your mouth, or I'll break your jaw." I meant it.

"Ouch. Someone's protective over his new toy." He had a stupid mocking grin plastered onto his face. "By the way, since when do we secretly hire new executives and give them huge-ass offices without consulting each other? Because I'm thinking of hiring Lucy here to be our new VP of Research and Development and giving her the office right next to mine." He slapped her ass cheeks hard as she cackled loudly.

"It was necessary to hire Amelia. She is advantageous to tracking down what we need." I was careful not to mention Tarun's name, just in case he tried to bribe any of the girls for information.

"I'm not complaining. She's a hot piece of ass that I don't mind seeing around the office." He tilted his head back and closed his eyes, as if replaying images of her in his mind.

I clenched my fist, ready to punch him in the face to get him to stop daydreaming of her.

"Now that I think of it, I haven't seen her around all week. Why is that?" he asked, opening his eyes and raising an eyebrow at me.

"She is reconsidering what I asked of her. She does not want to get caught up in anything…immoral," I replied.

I hadn't heard from her yet, so I wasn't sure of her decision. She was sweet and innocent. I understood why she hadn't taken the information I had shared with her well. I had offered her the opportunity to help us or walk away from the company. Walking away would probably be best for her. She had signed an NDA, so I knew she wouldn't share any of the information that she had learned. Still, I couldn't help feeling agitated whenever I considered the idea of her leaving.

"Let her go. We'll just have one of our guys take over the new feature," Jai said.

"She knows it best. It would be in our best interest to have her on board." If she didn't call me soon, I'd have to pay a visit to her apartment to convince her otherwise. Perhaps it would be more fun if she didn't call me.

"Forget about her for tonight," he told me. "Tara, my brother needs to loosen up," he said to one of the girls dancing near me.

I took a sip from my glass and let the smooth liquid warm my throat. Tara slinked her way to my seat. Her long black hair flowed past her fake tits and ended right above her belly-button piercing. Her body shimmered in the darkness from glitter or whatever she had used to highlight her skin.

She licked her lips as she neared me and swung her foot over my lap and onto the side of the seat of my chair, exposing her inner thigh to me. I was enveloped in a cloud of cheap perfume that smelled overly sweet, like cotton candy. She bent over her knee slightly while arching her back and slid her hands from her calves up to the top of her legs. One of her hands lingered over her G-string and pressed against her pussy through the fabric as she moved to the music.

Just then, my phone vibrated in my pocket. I pulled it out and stared at the screen in surprise. *Amelia.* I rose from my chair, pushing Tara off me as I walked to the hallway outside of the suite. I answered on the second ring.

"This is Shyam." There was no response from the other end, just a lot of noise, like she was in a busy place with a lot of people. But I knew she was there because I heard her breathing over the phone.

After a beat, she spoke. "I want a letter of recommendation." Her voice wavered as she said it, not sounding anything like the sweet purr that I was used to hearing from her. She sounded like she had been drinking.

"What?" I asked gruffly, annoyed that she was out somewhere, drunk.

"I want a letter of recommendation in return for helping you track down Tarun." Her voice carried stronger this time. She'd made her decision, and I felt relieved. But it wasn't smart of her to use Tarun's name in public. Prying ears were everywhere in the underworld. She should have known better after seeing the map of data in the computer lab.

"Where are you?" I changed the subject to keep her from exposing anything further than she already had.

"A hallway," she answered hesitantly.

I smirked to myself, remembering the last time I found her in a hallway. "Bad things happen to girls who spend time in hallways."

"Only when bad men find them in those hallways," she breathed into the phone. She remembered too.

"Jaan." *Dear.* "I'm the baddest of them all. Tell me. Where is this hallway?" She shouldn't have been out and intoxicated. Any jerk could take advantage of her in a vulnerable state.

"In a bar," she answered coyly.

I could already tell I wasn't going to get specifics out of her, but I asked anyway. "Where?"

"I'm not telling you." It was cute that she thought she could keep anything from me. I had my own ways of finding out what I needed to know.

"Stay there," I commanded her and hung up before she could argue.

I tracked her location using Sethi Tech tracking software and found her at a bar not too far from her apartment. I was certain she'd try to walk home inebriated and put herself at risk for assault.

I left the club through the private back entrance. The valet brought my car around. I shifted gears and sped away into the New York night.

XV. Amelia

"Stay there." *Click*. The line went dead.

Shit. Why did I have a feeling that he was tracking my location at this very moment? Soon, he'd show up here and I'd lose all the nerve I had built up just to make that phone call. One look at him and I knew I'd lose my resolve to hold out for my demands.

A text popped up on my screen. *Are you okay?* It was Nat. I must have been gone for a while if she was worried.

I tapped my reply to her. *All good. Just needed a breather.*

Oh, OK. I'm going to head out with Rob. Want me to walk you home first?

No. I'm OK. Go ahead. Have fun.

K. Luv you! XOXO

Luv you, too!

I had forgotten to ask if Josh was still out there too. I really didn't feel like seeing him again.

I returned to the bar and glanced around the area. No Josh. Now I just needed to avoid Shyam too. I grabbed my coat from the barstool and wrapped it around myself over my black tank top and skinny jeans, then stepped outside into the brisk night to make my way home before Shyam showed up.

A black sports car with tinted windows drove up to the curb in front of the bar. The driver's side door opened, and a tall and tanned figure stepped out. *Too late*. Shyam made his way around the front of the car and stalked toward me.

God, he looked good. His black collared shirt hugged his tight muscles. His sleeves were rolled up, revealing his muscular forearms. Dark jeans hung low on his hips. My eyes lazily roamed just below his hips to his crotch. I realized too late that I was gawking and quickly righted my gaze up to his face. A knowing smirk lit up his sexy face. This man was a fucking Indian god, and he knew it.

"Get in," he ordered as he opened the passenger-side door.

"I can walk home." I continued walking past him. Since the universe wouldn't allow me to preserve my ego around this man, I stumbled on a chunk of uneven pavement.

His hands quickly grabbed me before my butt met the sidewalk. "You're drunk. Get in the car. Now."

"I live one block over. I'll be fine," I said as I found enough balance to stand on my own.

"I don't take well to repeating myself. Get your ass in the car before I put you inside."

I sighed in resignation. *Fine.* I walked back to the car and sulked into the seat. Shyam got into the driver's seat and put the car in drive. He drove in silence, with his hand gripping the gearshift. His frustration with me showed in the white of his knuckles.

When we were alongside the front of my building, Shyam didn't stop the car. He kept driving past it.

"Hey! We missed my building," I said, pointing backward.

He stayed silent.

I raised my voice to get his attention. "Stop! Where are you going?"

"Somewhere to sober you up," he said, his eyes still focused on the road.

I stopped arguing, knowing that it was pointless to do so with Shyam. Turning my head to peer out of the passenger window, I took in the high rises and the soft glow of the New York City lights. They hypnotized me, steadying my thoughts. I felt myself drift off with the gentle vibration of the car and surrendered to the effects of the alcohol. The smell of cologne and tobacco soothed me to sleep.

I didn't know how long I had slept for, but when I awoke, the city lights I was accustomed to had disappeared. There were no buildings in sight, nor pedestrians walking on the street. The road was dark and eerie. Trees lined it, but instead of looking peaceful and welcoming, they seemed foreboding and haunting.

We approached a massive metal gate. It was impenetrable. Shyam braked the car, and the gate slid open, allowing us passage. Large flood lights lit the driveway to what looked like a fortress. It was basically a cement building with darkened windows, no ornate architecture or elaborate landscaping.

"Where are we?" I asked.

"My home away from home," he answered.

How could anyone live here? It looked so...cold.

We pulled into an underground garage with bright lights shining overhead. I had to squint through the brightness to make out the various sleek cars that decorated the lot. Shyam pulled his car into a spot between a yellow Lamborghini and a white Maserati. I was not surprised that he would own so many expensive cars but work in a city where driving them was nearly impossible. *Wealthy tech CEOs and their toys.*

He moved to the passenger side and opened my door. Apparently, chivalry wasn't dead, even if you were a criminal. I stepped out of the car and grabbed onto the door handle to steady myself. My brain still felt groggy, despite my mini nap. Shyam grasped my hand in his for support as he led me through the garage. Sparks flew up my arm from his touch, waking up my clouded brain. Anytime our skin made contact, I felt the energy of our chemistry.

We reached an industrial door with a retina scanner on the side of it. Shyam lowered his head and the door slid open, revealing an elevator. I stepped over the threshold, still holding his hand. Looking down at our joined hands, I noticed how our fingers had become intertwined unintentionally. He wasn't just holding *my* hand anymore; I was holding *his* in return. He caught me staring at our union, and my cheeks reddened with my embarrassment that he'd caught me. I felt him give my hand a gentle squeeze—reassurance that he wanted this too.

The doors opened, revealing a spacious living area with black marble floors. Gray leather couches lined the perimeter. Two sleek, low-lying wood coffee tables lay centered between the couches. A fireplace warmed the space in front of the couches. The interior looked nothing like the plain exterior of the home.

Expansive windows lined the far wall. I left Shyam's grasp and walked over to see the view. The sky was unusually dark for New York. I hadn't seen dark skies like this since I moved from the Pacific Northwest. Stars dusted the charcoal sky. It was beautiful.

"How far away are we from the city?" I asked.

"About ninety minutes," he replied while busying himself in the kitchen just off to the left of the living room. With the open floor plan, I could see through into the kitchen, which was just as sleek and masculine as the living room.

"Do you drive to work from here every day?" That commute must be so long, even if he used a driver.

"No, I have a place in the city that I use during the week. I come here on weekends for privacy."

Privacy for work or pleasure? I imagined he would want privacy for his illegal dealings, but maybe he brought other women here too. A flash of irritation coursed through me. Images of the bimbo fawning all over him the other night at Nirvana played like a movie on a screen in my head.

Shaking my head to stop my thoughts, I came back to reality. He was a gorgeous and powerful man, so it was stupid to think that he was a celibate monk in his spare time. Yet, I couldn't stop the bitterness I felt at the idea of him with another woman.

He returned to my side and offered me a teacup, one eyebrow raised. He studied my face as if he could read my thoughts. He witnessed the wheels turning in my head. "Where did you go, Amelia?"

I ignored his question. The last thing he needed to think was that I was some jealous girl pining for her hunky boss.

I took the cup into my hands and inhaled its warming scent. The spiced aroma soothed my senses. I took a sip, and notes of cinnamon and ginger warmed me on the way down. I felt my head clearing from its effects, my sanity returning.

"This is delicious. What is it?" I asked. I licked my lips slowly to clean off the milky foam that stuck to them. Shyam's eyes focused on my mouth, unwilling to look away. His lids were heavy with desire.

After a moment, he cleared his throat and replied, "Masala chai." His gaze lifted.

"This tastes nothing like the chai I get from Starbucks. It's so much better." I took another sip, savoring the taste.

"That stuff is fake and overly processed. This is my mother's recipe. She used to make it for us when we stayed up late studying in high school."

I was interested to hear about his upbringing and suspected he didn't share much of it with strangers. "Did you go to high school in America?"

"No. India," he replied.

I had heard stories about the education system in India from my friends in the industry and it sounded intense. I imagined that Shyam and Jai must have spent a lot of late nights studying to pass their exams.

"Is that where your mom lives now?" I asked, finishing off my chai and placing the cup on a nearby table.

His demeanor changed and he looked away. "She was killed five years ago."

My heart lurched in my chest for him. I reached for his hand. His gaze met mine again, touched by my gesture. "I'm so sorry. I didn't know."

"Jai and I were abroad in America when it happened. He was twenty-four and had just graduated from Stanford with his master's degree. I had already started working in the family business, using my contacts from business school to expand our network in the States."

"How old were you?" I asked.

"Twenty-seven," he said.

I did the math. That would make him thirty-two right now. Our age difference should have surprised me, but I couldn't deny the connection I felt despite it.

"Do you know who did it?" I hoped he didn't think I was prying. I just wanted to understand his past.

He pulled his hand away from mine. I felt the loss immediately. Stepping closer to the window, his eyes focused far into the horizon even though it was dark outside. "Tarun. His men kidnapped her on her way home from the market and held her hostage. They took her when her maid was distracted with one of the vendors."

"Where did they take her?" I whispered in horror.

"To the basement of one of his factories. They took turns raping her and hung her after they had their fill." His voice never wavered, but his eyes still determinedly avoided mine.

"Jesus," I gasped, tears threatening to spill over. The vivid image of how his mother had suffered was making my stomach churn, and I swallowed down the bile that had risen into my mouth. I would die if anyone laid a hand on my own mother.

"Tarun left a note for my father with the coordinates to her body. He found her in a landfill. He never got over his grief and took his life to be with her." He stared intently at whatever held his focus outside of the window, most likely to avoid the look of pity in my eyes.

My heart broke for the man standing in front of me. He had closed himself off from anyone because of his own grief. He was the patriarch of his ever-diminishing family. All the responsibility to carry on the family legacy was on his shoulders. It was no wonder why he was so serious and intense all the time.

I moved behind him and placed a hand on the center of his back. I could feel the vibration of his heartbeat. His hard muscles relaxed under my touch. I slid my hand down soothingly, bringing it to the side of his waist, and rested my cheek against his back, letting my tears wet his shirt.

Shyam turned to face me and framed my face with his large hands. As his thumbs wiped away my tears, I saw the torment he had kept hidden over the past five years reflected in his beautiful hazel eyes. In that moment, I didn't see a criminal or a tech tycoon standing in front of me. I just saw a man with a bruised heart—a man that I wanted to protect from his own past. "We will make him pay for what he did," I whispered as I stared up at him.

His eyes softened with gratitude and his lips met mine, offering me a silent thank-you. His kiss was so tender that it contradicted his powerful exterior. It consumed every part of me. I dug my fingertips into his biceps to steady myself...*Because I am falling for this man.*

He deepened the kiss. I opened my lips to let him in. His tongue tasted my mouth with fervor. Our tender kiss became wild and reckless as my tongue met his with the same need. One of his hands slid into my hair above the nape of my neck. He yanked hard on the strands as he bit my bottom lip, drawing blood. His tongue soothed the sharp pain. I couldn't help but let a moan escape from my throat.

In one fell swoop, he lifted me in his arms, cradling me against his chest. I wrapped my arms around his neck to hold on as he carried me upstairs.

He carried me into what I assumed was his bedroom, with black walls illuminated by soft golden light from two bedside lamps. Lush green plants decorated the corners on either side of the bed. It felt like a dark jungle, and the man holding me was a feral predator about to consume his prey.

He laid me on his bed, with my head propped up by soft, luxurious pillows. He climbed on top of me, sealing his mouth over mine. I breathed him in as our lips crashed together. My fingers weaved into his hair to pull him closer. I never wanted him to stop.

He trailed kisses down my neck as he moved lower, until his mouth found my nipple. He bit down on it through my clothes. I yelped at the pain but felt the familiar ache between my legs, begging to be relieved. He grabbed the neckline of my tank top with both of his strong hands and ripped it in half, all the way down through the hem. He pulled my exposed bra cups down under my breasts, smoothing his palms over my flesh. While his tongue massaged my bare nipple, his hands moved to the button of my jeans, undoing it with deft fingers.

He pushed off of me and stood in front of the bed. I longed for him to return and encase me with his warmth, but he began working my shoes and socks off my feet instead. He gave each one a gentle kiss as he revealed undiscovered skin. My breath hitched every time his lips made contact. Then he peeled my jeans down my waist. I pushed my hips up in a bridge, allowing him to slide them down and off my legs.

He stepped back from the bed to take in the sight before him—me, with my cotton bra around my ribs, bare tits ready for him, and my arousal soaking through my matching white panties. *Why couldn't I have worn something sexier tonight?* I clamped my knees together to hide my pedestrian panties.

"Open them," he commanded.

I did as he said, letting my knees fall apart, opening wide for him. His eyes shone with approval. Keeping them glued to me, he worked the buttons of his shirt and discarded it onto the floor. His chiseled abs and arms were ripped like stone.

He stepped out of his shoes and removed his socks, kicking them away. My eyes roamed to the deep V cut of his hips that pointed to the protrusion in his pants. He undid his fly and pushed them along with his boxers down to the floor, revealing his long, thick dick. So smooth and already oozing precum at the tip. *Oh God.* I licked my lips as the image burned my eyes—so hot, like the sun. My legs parted wider in response to what I was seeing. I could feel my wetness dripping down the sides of my panties.

He inched closer to the bed like he was hunting me down, guided by the scent of my arousal. Perching himself at the foot of the bed, he pressed my thighs down with his palms. He buried his nose into my panty-covered pussy, inhaling deeply. My breathing grew ragged with anticipation. He released his hold on my thighs. He caught the edge of my panties in his mouth and tugged them down, pulling them off with only his teeth. Like a beast ripping away flesh with its fangs. Everything he did was with raw animal intention.

He pressed kisses on my inner thigh until he reached my pussy. He licked my slit, causing my back to arch off the mattress at the shock of pleasure.

"You're wet for me already, *jaan*," he whispered against my folds before devouring me. The pressure building between my legs was so painful. I needed release. I wanted him inside of me. I grabbed his head with my hands and pulled his face up to mine, raising my pelvis to meet his.

"So impatient," he said before he kissed me, letting me taste my arousal on his tongue. "If you don't stay still, I'll have to tie up those hands. Maybe you'd prefer that?"

I had never been tied up in bed before, but something told me I would love whatever he did to me. He had such control over my body.

He continued his torturous assault on my pussy with his mouth. He moved to my clit, sucking my nub between his teeth, and biting down. Pain flashed in my clit, causing me to cry out. He soothed the pain with his tongue, massaging it with gentle strokes. Blood rushed to my area, which only heightened my pleasure, to my surprise. His tongue lapped at my slit as his thumb took over massaging my nub in rhythmic circles. I felt my pelvic muscles clench. Sweat coated my body. My hands fisted his hair, holding on for dear life.

"Oh God," I moaned loudly. My body convulsed in waves of pleasure as I found my release.

I lay limp on the bed, trying to catch my breath. I was in disbelief of what had just happened. I had never come so hard in my life.

Shyam rose from between my legs, his lips wet with my arousal. His dick was so hard that its vein protruded like it was about to burst. I had never been with a man who enjoyed going down on me as much as he seemed to.

He kissed the valley between my breasts before moving up to my neck. Small bites nipped at my neck. I felt my toes curl and my body tense with pleasure. *How can I still be so turned on?*

"We're not finished yet," he hummed in my ear and sucked my lobe. He moved to my mouth, abusing me with his kisses. His dick pressed into my belly, wetting my skin with precum. I slid my hand between us and stroked him. I wanted his wetness all over me. To mark me. His gaze went from confident sex god to heavy-lidded and in need of his own release. I fed off his desire for me. I relished pulling this controlled man over the edge with me.

"I need you, Shyam," I breathed into his face. I hooked my legs around his ass to urge him into me. He couldn't resist. I felt the head of his cock press into me.

"Wait! You're not wearing anything!" I had almost lost myself in the moment and become irresponsible. I was on the pill, but we hadn't talked about our sexual history.

"No. I want all of you," he growled. Sensing my nervousness, he reassured me, "I'm clean. Are you?"

I nodded.

"Do you trust me?" his eyes probed me.

I do. "Yes."

His dick pressed through my inner folds. He was so large that I tensed up as he filled me.

"Breathe, Amelia," he whispered, coaxing me with a passionate kiss. I exhaled into his mouth and relaxed my muscles, allowing him to slide through my cream.

It was the first time I had had anyone in me without a barrier. The sensation was so much more intense than what I was used to.

He rested inside of me for only a couple of seconds, giving me a chance to stretch to his size before drawing out. Before I had a chance to mourn the loss of him, he slammed back into me with such force that the headboard banged into the wall behind us. He pumped into me faster, his balls slapping against my ass.

I felt my muscles tighten again. I couldn't believe I was coming again so soon. "I can't believe—"

I couldn't finish my sentence before I exploded into pieces. "Shyam," I cried out as my pleasure peaked.

He fucked me harder than before as his cock thickened inside of me. "*Jaan*," he shouted as he filled me with his cum.

He collapsed onto me with his face buried into my neck. My arms snaked around his back, holding him tight. We lay there for a while, sticky with sweat and arousal.

When his cock fully softened, he pulled out and rolled onto his back next to me. The only sound between us was our breaths falling into a steady resting pace. He stared up at the ceiling. "Did I hurt you?"

"A little," I replied. *But I liked it.* It was the best sex of my life.

The mattress shifted under his weight as he got up from the bed. He walked over to the opposite side and took my hand to guide me off the bed too. Warm cum slid down my thigh as gravity took over.

He led me into the bathroom and into the shower. The warm water from the dual heads felt so good on my spent body. The view in front of me wasn't bad either.

Streams of water flowed down his chiseled pecs and six pack. His biceps flexed as he lathered his torso with soap. He had emptied himself into me just minutes ago and his flaccid dick still looked big. I felt my mouth water as small soap bubbles slid down his shaft. Realizing I was gawking again, I grabbed a bottle of shampoo to break my focus.

"Let me." He took the bottle from me and squeezed some onto his large palm. "Turn around."

I turned, giving him access to my hair. *Oh.* Long fingers weaved themselves into my hair and massaged my scalp. I tilted my head back further, enjoying the sensation of being taken care of by a man. He carefully washed my hair and smoothed on conditioner. Soapy hands rubbed my neck and back. They roamed my entire body, slipping down to my ass cheeks and snaking around to my front. He lathered my breasts in gentle circles and moved down my belly toward my folds. The water washed away the suds from my body. His fingers found my clit, and instinctively, I rocked against them. He worked my sweet spot in languid strokes.

Any memory of the soreness from earlier disappeared as arousal took over. I backed up into his frame, feeling his hard cock press into my skin. He alternated kisses and bites down my neck and shoulder.

I turned my face back to find his lips and was met with a hungry welcome. Our tongues caressed each other as I ground into his hand.

"Hold onto me," he groaned in my ear. He spun me around to face him. Suddenly, he lifted me off the floor and pressed me against the shower wall. I wrapped my legs around his hips, hooking my ankles together behind him. My arms wrapped around the back of his neck tightly.

He invaded me, penetrating me with his fullness. I moaned with pleasure. I didn't think I could ever get used to his size. He pounded into me, my ass pressing into the wall behind me. I couldn't tell if it was the steam or lust that clouded my vision.

His teeth latched onto my neck, biting so hard that I would have marks tomorrow. His marks. The idea of the world seeing his marks of ownership turned me on even more.

I felt my pussy grow slicker with every pump he administered. Waves of heat coursed through my belly. I couldn't hold on anymore. Pleasure overtook my body, reverberating through my core. His pace quickened and his cock stiffened even more before he found his release.

Pressed to the wall, I unhooked my legs and let them fall with the weight of gravity to the floor. They felt like jelly. I had to hold on to his shoulders for support.

I found his beautiful eyes with mine. They were usually fixed with a stern expression, but now only gentleness reflected in them. I got lost in this softer side of him.

We rinsed off under the now cool water and dried off with fluffy oversized towels. Back in his bedroom, Shyam slipped on a pair of boxers.

I wasn't sure what would happen next. I wanted to spend the night with him, but I thought maybe it was more appropriate to head home. I knew we had shared something special this evening, but I didn't want to assume what we had done was anything more. I picked up my panties from the floor and slid them on.

I moved to slide on my jeans, when Shyam interrupted me. "What do you think you're doing?"

"Getting dressed. I can call an Uber to drop me home," I replied.

He opened his top dresser drawer and pulled out one of his t-shirts and tossed it to me. "Put this on."

I dropped my jeans and pulled the oversized shirt over my head.

He pulled back the sheets. "Get in."

He wanted me to stay. I tried to contain my excitement as I slid into bed next to him.

Inwardly, I was smiling because he probably didn't view this as a booty call either. He tucked me into his body, so his front cradled my back. His heavy arm anchored me down to the bed. I relaxed into his warm hold and felt his breathing even out behind me. Not too long after, I was lulled into a deep sleep too.

XVI. Amelia

I woke the next morning to sunlight shining through the windows. I rolled over to push myself up to sit. My head pounded. *Fuck. Why did I drink so much last night?* I'd been asking myself that question a lot lately.

I rubbed the sleep from my eyes, and my surroundings came into focus. This wasn't my apartment.

Memories of last night flooded my brain. The bar. Drinks. Some annoying guy trying to get into my pants. A very sexy guy actually getting into my pants.

I looked down and saw the huge t-shirt I was wearing, with just panties underneath. *I had sex with Shyam!* It wasn't a dream.

The bed was empty. I looked to the nightstand for the time and found two tablets and a glass of water next to the bed. Pain relievers. I gulped them down with desperation.

The scent of bacon lured me out of the bedroom. I hadn't eaten dinner last night, and my stomach grumbled to remind me of it. I was sure my hair was a damn mess and I had morning breath, but I was too hungry to care.

I followed my nose downstairs to the kitchen. Shyam stood in front of the stove in a t-shirt and low-slung jeans that hugged his tight ass. He turned to look at me.

"Hungry?" he asked, scooping eggs onto a plate.

My belly let out another loud growl. I grabbed my midsection to quiet the noise. "I skipped dinner last night," I replied.

He grinned at my defensiveness.

He set the plates on the kitchen island, which was ready with cutlery and cloth napkins—one plate with scrambled eggs, bacon, and toast and another with egg whites and spinach.

I pulled out a barstool in front of the one with the bacon. "I call dibs on this one!"

"Good, because that one's for you." He placed a piping-hot cup of coffee in front of me and a protein shake in front of his plate.

I helped myself to an ample helping of sugar and cream from the glass serving tray. Everything he did oozed class. It constantly surprised me that a drug lord could be so well-mannered.

I cupped my coffee mug with my hands to absorb its warmth. "That's the most boring breakfast I've ever seen."

He smirked. "How else do you think I get those abs that you love so much?"

I blushed hard, reliving last night. His abs really were so cut. I wanted to run my tongue along them now, just to get a taste.

112

I cleared my throat to change the subject. "I never have time for breakfast. I'm always rushing out of the door in the morning."

"How come?" he asked, taking a bite of his omelet.

"I go to bed late," I replied between nibbles of bacon. "I like coding through the night. I get my best work done after midnight." I didn't have the best diet. I pretty much just ate whatever I could find in my fridge or order as takeout from a nearby restaurant.

"That must be a developer quirk," he said.

"Quirk?" I asked.

"When Jai was in high school, he used to stay up until dawn coding because he loved it so much," he said as he wiped his mouth with his napkin.

"I guess we're all night owls." There was nothing like programming at night. The rest of the world was asleep, so there were no interruptions while I worked. I felt that I could think clearer in the night. If it weren't for work, I would probably stay up all night to code for fun and sleep all day.

I stared at his healthy breakfast. "Are you a vegetarian?" I asked.

"What makes you think that?"

"Aren't a lot of people from India vegetarian?" I'd had a few Indian friends in college who were strict vegetarians, so I was aware that it was common for the culture.

"Most are. The ones that do eat meat don't eat beef or pork. Well, in your case, bacon." He winked at me.

"Why do you have it in your fridge, then?" I was genuinely curious and extremely glad that he had bacon in his fridge.

"I used to be vegetarian when I lived in India. But the minute Jai and I moved here, we decided it was more fun to sin after tasting our first bacon burgers."

I giggled. I couldn't imagine Shyam scarfing down a bacon burger like a hungry college kid. He seemed too proper to eat one.

"I'm guessing no bacon burgers now?" I motioned at his abs with my chin. Those weren't the abs of a man who lived off burgers.

"We went overboard when we first cheated on our vegetarianism, but they're not so great for you." He made an uncomfortable face in mockery as he smoothed his hands down his torso.

This was the first time we had engaged in light-hearted conversation. Our relationship, whatever it was, had changed. He was opening up to me more, and I subsequently felt less shy around him. I enjoyed this dynamic, since I had only ever experienced Shyam's intensity. His exterior still intimidated me, but now his eyes glowed with a lightness that made him more approachable.

Shyam finished his food and cleared his plate into the sink. I continued to enjoy my breakfast.

He turned around and leaned against the sink, with his hands gripping either side of it. "Tell me more about this letter of recommendation you want from me."

I took a long sip of my coffee to collect my memories of what I had demanded last night. I wasn't sure how to negotiate the letter I wanted in exchange for helping him. Hearing about how Tarun had raped and murdered his mother made me yearn to help, but I still wanted something in return for risking my career by engaging in illegal activities. Essentially, the Sethi brothers were using me for something they needed, and I would use them right back.

Swallowing my coffee in a large gulp, I started, "Um. I never expected to work for a company engaged in—uh—illegal activities. Since the job you offered comes with risks, I think I deserve—uh—further compensation." That totally didn't come out as confident as I'd wanted it to.

He didn't laugh at me or put me down. Instead, he studied my face. "And you aren't asking for more money instead? Why a letter?" he asked, perplexed, as he crossed his arms.

I let out a big sigh and laid all my cards on the table. "Because I'm a woman in the tech industry, and it's really hard to climb the ladder because I'm not a man."

I felt like a manipulative person for demanding this, especially considering the reason why he was tracking Tarun. But I had to think about myself, too. Women in the workforce had been getting the short end of the stick for way too long, and the tech industry was no exception.

"And if you had a letter of recommendation from Sethi Tech, you could rise to the top," he said as those hazel eyes remained glued to me.

I nodded, hoping he wouldn't make fun of my ambition. Powerful men like him probably thought it was "cute" or "precious" when a woman showed drive and determination in her career.

He walked around the island to meet me. I turned my body to face him. Tipping my chin up with his finger so he could look me in my eyes, he said, "You don't need a letter of recommendation from me or anyone. You are brilliant and you deserve a senior position in any company. But if it's what you want, I will give it to you."

His confidence in me warmed me to my core. I struggled with having confidence in myself, but here was this man who believed in me and wanted me to succeed.

"Thank you," I said quietly.

He lowered his lips and gave me a gentle kiss on the side of my mouth. "You're welcome, *jaan*. Shall I give you a lift home?"

"Yes, please." I smiled.

XVII. Amelia

I resumed my position at Sethi Tech, despite the fact it had nothing to do with any of the details listed in my "official" job description. Most of my time was spent in the basement lab, formatting altered photos of an eighteen-year-old Tarun. I worked on creating as many possible images as I could to reflect how he would look today if someone captured a photo of him.

Today was an exception, and I was happy to be back in my office to take a breather from being alone in a secluded room.

Tracking Tarun had proved to be as difficult as Shyam had promised. It really was like the man didn't exist. No hits existed for any of the cloaked photo possibilities I had generated. I had even considered that he could be wearing prosthetics, but the possibilities were endless.

Jai and Shyam had found basic information about him, like his name, age, and schooling information, but those were all things that could be found without using highly developed tracking software. I needed to find out something more substantial than breadcrumbs of information.

My search had become personal. I couldn't imagine the anguish that Shyam must have suffered when his mother was so brutally killed. I had seen the pain in his eyes when he'd shared his burden with me. It had to have been hard for a man as guarded as he was to let down his walls. He still kept up his hard shell around me, especially at the office, but I had witnessed the cracks. I still felt special that he had chosen to share any of his past with me, and I would do anything I could to help him get revenge.

After that night at his house, we hadn't had sex again. I saw him at the office, but he was mostly in boss mode, though his approach with me was softer than before. He didn't hesitate to issue commands when it came to the search, but every so often, he'd caress my cheek or pull me in for a soft kiss to ease the blow of his demands. The heat of our chemistry took over after those small bits of affection, which led to lots of making out and over-the-clothing groping. We were always interrupted, with Shyam leaving to put out more fires from Tarun sabotaging his business.

The damage to his business had put a strain on him, and he seemed worried, though he tried to hide it under his composed front. I could tell that it was wearing him down.

I still didn't know what we were, but our relationship had changed. I cared a lot about Shyam, and I was pretty sure he cared about me. He had even started sending a car to my apartment to take me to work and back home. I had argued with him about it because I preferred to walk but had ultimately given in because he was too stubborn to change his mind. I guess it came in handy, since it had been cold and rainy most days lately.

I was brainstorming about possible new search parameters when my phone buzzed. *Hey, bitch! Where have you been all my life?*

I texted back. *Hey, Nat! At work.*

New job? Or old job with Mr. Sexy, I mean, Mr. Sethi? :-p

Very funny! How's Rob?

Who? She went through guys so quickly that it didn't surprise me that she had forgotten the bar-guy's name.

That guy you left the bar with!

Ohhh. He was OK. Too quick in bed. I ended up ordering pizza after he left and watched some Netflix. Typical Nat. Love 'em and leave 'em.

Her sex-life moved too fast for me to follow. Even if Rob had been a good lay, she would have moved on by now. She liked being non-committal, with no one to answer to.

I continued typing. *Better luck next time!*

Maybe. Where'd you wander off to that night?

Shyam picked me up.

What?!?!?!?! And I'm just finding out?! Did you bone?

I smiled, remembering his kisses and his touch. *I don't kiss and tell.*

That means YES! You naughty girl! How was it? Did he tie you up and do dirty shit to you?

119

What?! No to tying up. I didn't want to go into details about how Shyam had fucked me relentlessly until I was sore. That was my memory to enjoy. And I did *enjoy* it, in the privacy of my home, under the sheets, when I was alone.

So, YES to dirty shit? She wasn't going to let this go.

Define "dirty shit".

YASSSSSS! He's treating you good, though? She was always a big sister looking out for me.

You don't need to worry about anything. I was sure that this relationship meant something to Shyam too.

You know I can't help it. You decided to stay at the company? Make sure you look out for yourself, first and foremost.

Always. Love you.

Love you, too. Dinner soon? I need details!

Yes, please!

"Texting on the job?" Jai said as he leaned against my door frame, looking in at me. I didn't know how long he had been there spying on me.

Startled, I immediately locked my phone screen and dropped it. It landed with a clatter on my desk.

"Careful, before the bosses have you written up for that," he teased.

His frame was slightly shorter than Shyam's yet still lean, but his boyish smile always hinted at mischief. I imagined that the ladies threw themselves at him. He was the more approachable Sethi brother.

I knew he was joking, so I went along with it. "Are you going to make Jessica from HR lecture me for four more hours?"

He chuckled and closed my office door, then plopped down into the chair facing my desk and crossed one ankle over his knee. "Any progress on the search?"

I released a big sigh and slouched in my chair. I assumed by now Jai knew that Shyam had confided in me the real reason they needed data-tracking apps.

"I feel you on that," he said to console me.

"I just don't understand how a person can be completely invisible today. Everyone has some sort of personal data or current photo stored somewhere. It's like he lives under a rock."

"I wouldn't be surprised if he did, literally. He went into hiding recently, but even before, that he had been elusive when it came to data. Trust me. We've been at this for years, and we're just as stumped as you are."

"You said he had a brother. Did you find any data on him? Maybe we can find something that connects them. Any photos of him?" If there were any photos of his brother, then I was sure we could use them to find a hit. Siblings often shared a similar facial feature or two, so it was possible that the software could pick up on those similarities.

"There's not much on him, either. Just old information and photos like with Tarun. Their IT team did one hell of a job concealing them. He died not too long ago, and obviously, nothing new has surfaced on him since then." He had taken out his phone and searched through it as he spoke. "Here."

I took it from him. It was a photo of a brown-skinned man, bruised and bloodied. He looked to be about Jai's age, late twenties. His face was round, like in the old photo of Tarun that I had seen, but it wasn't as full. He was missing the birthmark that Tarun had on his neck. The eyes were also close-set like Tarun's, but they were closed. He was dead.

"Scroll to the next one."

I swiped my finger and another photo appeared. It was another Indian man but with lighter skin, and even heavier set than the last one. This man was alive and not beaten. He had light-brown eyes and looked different from the previous man that I had seen. The only thing that was the same were his narrowly set eyes.

"What am I looking at now?" I asked, confused.

"That's also Tarun's brother."

I stared at the picture in disbelief. *Prosthetics.* He must have been wearing heavy prosthetics in the second photo to change his appearance.

"The same one?! That's insane. He looks so different."

"He had been working in our network in New York in disguise. We stripped his prosthetics after he died to see what he really looked like. Then we took the first photo you saw. The second photo is one we captured when he was alive and in disguise. I was hoping we could get a hit using either of these photos, but we had no luck with older versions of facial-recognition software." He took the phone back from me when I offered it to him. "They are already uploaded to our shared cloud for your use. Since your software has higher accuracy for people of color and accounts for cloaking, I know we'll have a higher chance of finding Tarun using it."

It all made sense. We just needed someone to take a current photo of Tarun and compare it to photos of his brother with and without prosthetics for hits. The photo captured would carry the coordinates of where the photo was taken too, so we would be able to track him down. It sounded simple, but Tarun was an expert at hiding.

"How did his brother die?" I asked Jai to piece together more information about our enemy.

Silence. He just stared at me, but his eyes conveyed everything I needed to know.

"Never mind," I said, dropping my gaze and shaking my head. I didn't need to hear the words to know that Shyam and Jai had killed him.

He lowered his voice to a more serious tone. "You know what we do. We're not spoiled corporate chumps who spend our time on the golf course or sailing yachts. We're dangerous men who work hard for our money. You need to come to terms with that if you're going to be Shyam's girlfriend."

This was the first time he had addressed my relationship with his brother. I didn't know how much he knew about our intimate relationship, but I assumed brothers talked.

"I'm not sure we're together in that way, so to speak." I didn't feel comfortable sharing much, so I didn't elaborate any further.

"Really? Because he kept you his little secret when you started here. He's never been shy about his other women, but he's been surprisingly tight-lipped about you."

"His other women?" I repeated quietly. For all I knew, he could be seeing other women in addition to me. We had never discussed being exclusive, so it would be fair if he slept with other women, but the idea made my stomach drop.

"Well, the other *past* women. I haven't seen him with anyone else since you came around. Except last Friday, with that stripper."

Last Friday? That was the night he had told me about his parents and then taken me completely. *Was he with another woman when I called him from the bar?* He'd fucked me without protection after her. I felt sick to my stomach. I tasted bile in my mouth.

Jai's phone buzzed with a text. He focused on his screen, seemingly oblivious to the tears of anger that threatened to fall from my eyes.

"Oh shit. Gotta go, love. Drug-dealer emergency." He rushed out of my office to sort out whatever needed his attention, leaving me alone to stew in my dread.

XVIII. Shyam

Ten fucking crates of product—all intercepted. My men prepared the shipment and loaded it onto the cargo ship for delivery. When the cargo arrived at the port in Barcelona, our crates had been emptied, leaving only the computer hardware we used to hide our product. We were able to hack into the video security system used at both ports, but nothing suspicious was discovered from the footage.

Our client was livid. They assumed that we were responsible for the loss and were taking advantage of them, but I had had my most trustworthy men work this job, so I knew they weren't responsible for what had happened. Someone had sabotaged our shipment, and my gut led me to one culprit—Tarun.

We couldn't continue doing business like this. Every shipment we sent out was at risk of being stolen or destroyed. We had lost our client in Barcelona because of it. They had been our major distributor in Spain, and our stronghold within the country was now destroyed. No doubt they had already moved on to sign a contract with Tarun and his men. This shit would keep happening until we destroyed Tarun. There was absolutely no way we could both continue to conduct business while the other was alive, and I had no plans on dying anytime soon. I was impatient, and I needed Jai and Amelia to locate him *now*.

Jai entered our suite at Nirvana just after I had finished getting details about the raid. It was daytime, so the club was closed to the public, and our employees had yet to clock in to start prepping for the evening. The suite was more private than my office at Sethi Tech to discuss our next steps.

"What took you so long?" I barked at him.

I was fed up with his tardiness whenever shit hit the fan. I had always excused it before because he was a genius. Without him, our business wouldn't have thrived the way it had before Tarun started meddling in our affairs. But Jai was aware of his brilliance too, and his ego made him think the world revolved around him.

I was the opposite. I was always prompt to meetings, if not early. I hated waiting on him, and with how much rage was bubbling in me right now, I wasn't too shy to kick his ass to teach him a lesson.

"Relax. I'm here now," he shot back. He took the seat across from me, facing my desk.

"Our business is up in smoke and you're waltzing in here like it's no big deal." I was annoyed and ready to strike at anyone in my line of fire. It was probably a good thing we were here instead of at the office, where I'd probably have lashed out at innocent employees.

"Shut the fuck up. You know I care. Why else would I be here now?" he said in an attempt to placate me in his immature, brotherly way. "I was with your girlfriend at the office."

I knew who he was talking about. My curiosity was piqued; I felt a pang of desire whenever I heard anyone refer to her at the office. However, when my brother mentioned her, it was usually to get a rise out of me, and I never let him down. "She's not my girlfriend."

His eyebrow raised with skepticism. "You sure about that? You seem to be overly sensitive when it comes to her."

"She's vital to locating Tarun. That's all. It's not like I can depend on you to do it on your own." I knew it was a low blow, but he had pushed a button, and I was not in the mood to be harassed.

"I don't know why you won't just admit that you care about her. You damn near ripped apart her office when you saw me talking to her on her first day."

"I don't know what you're talking about," I said, brushing him off.

"I get it, man," he continued. "She's beautiful, smart, and has a sweet personality."

"Sweet? Since when do you use the word 'sweet'?" I mocked.

"You know what I mean. She's innocent. I get the appeal. Hell, if you weren't with her, I'd try to hit it." He leaned back in his chair, flashing his cheesiest lover-boy smile.

I growled at his statement. I didn't *do* girlfriends, but she was mine to be whatever I wanted her to be until I was done. "Drop it," I snarled.

"Fine. But it speaks volumes, how worked up you are right now. I've never seen you this way over a woman. Not even Salena."

I knew he'd bring Salena up. She was the daughter of a former distributor. Our fathers had made the arrangement for our marriage. I never wanted to get married, but I didn't have a say in the matter, until my father passed away. Breaking the contract that our fathers had set in place had angered Salena's father and caused him to place his loyalties with Tarun. We fell out of contact after I broke things off.

I sighed in resignation. "Look, we need her if we want to take Tarun down before he destroys our business any further."

"You don't love her, do you?" he pressed, disregarding my denial.

"What?!" I nearly fell out of my chair. He had to be joking. I didn't do *love.* I had always admired my parents' marriage. They had had an arranged marriage but had developed feelings for each other as the years had carried on. The fact that they had loved each other so much, right up to their dying days, had shaped my view of marriage as something that was to be taken seriously.

I didn't love Salena when we were engaged, but I thought it would come with time. I soon found out I wasn't made for that type of commitment. I was the biggest criminal in North America and liked to fuck whenever and wherever I wanted. I had too much respect for the sanctity of marriage to tarnish it with my lifestyle. If I were ever to settle down, I would respect my significant other too much to put her through what my mother had endured while she was married to my father. His lifestyle had killed her. She hadn't deserved the death she had received.

I lusted after Amelia. She had a way of disarming me. It was why I had shared my past with her, and for her to understand why I needed her help with tracking Tarun. I had never told another woman about how my parents had died and my need for revenge, but I had felt that it was necessary to share my past to get her invested in our cause.

I had thought that if I fucked her once, I'd have my fill and get my need out of my system. But instead, I wanted more. I had never tasted pussy like hers before. So sweet and smooth. Thoughts of her coming around my dick and screaming my name distracted me at the office. I was hard anytime I thought of her. I couldn't resist her lips when I saw her during the day.

But I refused to ever be that man who settled down with one woman. I had had that arrangement once before, and I had sworn I would never do it again. I planned to continue my life in the underworld until the day I left this Earth. I would fuck around as much as I wanted. I would never do that behind a girlfriend or wife's back. I wasn't a cheater, and I refused to sneak around behind my woman's back to get pussy.

So, no, I would never *love* Amelia.

Seeing my shock, Jai replied, "Okay, okay. I see from your reaction that I've hit a nerve. You should probably let her know that you don't love her, if it's really true."

"Why?" I was confused.

"When I was with her, I mentioned that stripper you were cozying up to last week and she freaked out. She thought I didn't see, but she was about to cry when I told her."

"What the fuck, Jai?" This was worse than I had anticipated. I hadn't fucked Tara, but Amelia probably assumed I had because of my brother's big mouth. We had never discussed seeing each other exclusively. I had thought it was understood that this was just a casual thing, but I must have misled her by treating her tenderly and letting her sleep over after our first night together. Now, I felt like I had to explain myself to Amelia. This was exactly why I didn't want a monogamous relationship. The frustration was giving me a migraine.

"How would I know she'd react that way? I didn't think she was in love with you or anything."

"Do me a favor. Stay out of it from now on. And stop running your mouth with her. Her only role that concerns you is 'employee,' nothing else."

"Yes, *bhaiya*." *Big brother*. He used to call me that when we were younger out of respect. Now, he used it whenever he felt like I was lecturing him too much.

"Now that we're done with the girl talk, we need to discuss saving our business." Tarun was going to die.

*****

Jai and I spent the rest of the day strategizing. We conference-called our men in India to fill them in. Our men would be ramping up security on pending shipments and chaperoning the shipments until they reached our clients.

We couldn't hold off any longer on finding Tarun. I needed him gone. The next step was a meeting with Amelia to discuss the facial-recognition software.

Amelia. Jai's words from earlier were seared in my mind.

I needed her for her programming skills, but I couldn't continue a sexual relationship with her if she was in love with me. This had to remain casual or we could have nothing at all. I wouldn't lead her on.

After finishing up at Nirvana, I texted her, saying that we needed to talk.

When she didn't reply, I called but reached her voicemail instead. I knew she was at home because she used the driver that I had arranged for her. I was livid that she was ignoring me, so I had my driver take me to her apartment.

In the car, I loosened the knot on my tie to ease the tension festering inside. I was angry at Tarun for everything he had done to sabotage my family and business. I was angry at Jai for running his mouth. I was angry at Amelia for ignoring me. I balled my hands into fists on my thighs, ready to punch something in my fury.

We pulled up to her building. It didn't have a doorman or a lobby. I didn't like the idea of her staying in a building without good security.

I knew the access code from the information I had found in her file from my men. I punched it in, unlocking the main door. I nearly yanked it off its hinges.

I stormed up to her door. The rage inside of me was spilling over. I banged on her door with my fist so loud that I was sure her neighbors had felt the floors shake.

I heard rustling inside and then footsteps approaching the door. The sounds paused for a moment. I knew she was looking at me through the peephole.

The locks clicked and then the door opened. Amelia stood in the doorway with her hand on the knob, ready to slam the door in my face. Her face said it all. She was just as pissed as I was, but for different reasons.

Her beautiful red hair was in a messy bun at the top of her head and her mascara was smudged. I could tell she had been crying because her eyes were red and swollen. She wore a thin white t-shirt with no bra underneath, and black yoga leggings that clung to her full hips. My cock stirred at what I saw through her shirt. Her nipples stood at attention underneath, as if her body were turned on at the mere sight of me, despite her heavy emotions.

133

"When I call, you answer the fucking phone. Understand?" My voice roared like thunder.

Her jaw dropped in shock. She was raging like a hurricane. "You have some nerve to come over here and yell at me," she hissed.

I was sure her neighbors had a front-row view of our confrontation, and I wasn't in the mood for an audience. I grabbed her waist with both hands and lifted her off the floor.

"Hey! Put me down!" She flailed her body to get me to loosen my grip.

I carried her inside and kicked the door shut. Her apartment was small, so her living room was the bedroom. I threw her down on the full-sized bed. She landed on her back with a bounce. I noticed the way her tits shook from the impact. She quickly planted her feet on the floor and righted herself, glaring at me, even more pissed than before.

"Where was your phone?" I had steadied my voice, but my anger was still evident.

She scoffed at me and put her hands on her hips. "Why do you care? Are your strippers not entertaining enough?" As if with satisfaction at her own scrappiness, she grinned. I admired her more when she was feisty. I liked it when she fought me.

"Actually, no. They're not."

She was surprised by my response. She must have expected me to raise my voice and deny her implications, but I was an expert at winning arguments. I changed my tactic. The element of surprise always gave one the upper hand in a disagreement. "Are you jealous of my extracurricular activities?"

I knew the answer from the way her face reddened. Jai was right. She might not necessarily love me, but she did have feelings for me, or she wouldn't have cared.

"No." Her reply was laced with untruth. I had to play this carefully. I needed to make her understand that this was a casual relationship for me. Nothing more.

I slowly closed the distance between us until I was close enough that her hard nipples poked me through our clothes. Angry and turned on was a great look on her.

I lowered my mouth to her ear. "Good. Then you wouldn't care if I left right now and rang a *friend* for company?" I hadn't been with another woman since I'd met her. She didn't need to know that, though, especially not now, when I was trying to convince her that *this* was nothing more than sex.

Her breath hitched as my nose tickled the spot on her neck right under her ear. "Don't fall for me, Amelia," I whispered. She pulled back and looked at me, her eyebrows furrowed. "I'm not a good man. I *will* hurt you."

Her eyes turned glassy at my warning as tears threatened to fall. I knew she understood.

I felt like a bastard for making her cry, but it was necessary. I needed to cut her off before she could argue with me for seeing strippers and revealing even more of her heart to me. Once it was all out in the open, it couldn't be taken back.

I had no intention of settling down, and she needed to understand that before her feelings got hurt further. She was a brilliant girl with the potential for a bright future, and her time shouldn't be spent pining for a bad guy like me.

I couldn't offer her my heart, but I could ease the pain of rejection. I reached out and wrapped my hand around her neck. I could feel her pulse accelerate from my touch. "You will answer the phone when I call you. Do you hear me?"

She nodded while my hand still clutched her neck. I needed to be able to get ahold at of her at any time for her own security. The work that she was doing for me was dangerous, and I had to be assured that she was safe. It was one of the reasons that I had a driver take her to and from work. She might not be my girlfriend, but I still worried for her safety. I had experience with Tarun's violence, when he had killed my mother, and for that reason, I was protective over Amelia.

"Apologize to me." I needed to hear that she respected my role in her life.

Blinking back her tears, she conceded. "I'm sorry," she whispered.

"Good girl. Now show me how sorry you are." I pushed on her neck and guided her weight down, causing her to fall to her knees.

She knew what I wanted. Her hands moved to my waistband, where she undid the fly of my pants. She pulled down my slacks, taking my boxers with them. My cock sprung out at full attention, ready for her mouth. Precum was already dripping from the head.

"Kiss me," I ordered her. She obeyed, pressing her lips lightly to my head. A thread of my precum followed her as she pulled away. Her lips glistened with my wetness. I couldn't hold back the groan that escaped me as she licked her lips to taste me.

"Open wide, *jaan.*" I moved my hand to grip the back of her head. Wild tendrils of red hair fell from her bun and onto her face. I guided my cock into her mouth, enjoying the feeling as I made contact with her warm tongue. She used it to massage the bottom of my shaft with slow pulses. Her beautiful green eyes rolled back in her head as I leaked more arousal into her mouth. It felt like heaven. The way she savored me made me feel like a king.

"Suck me," I commanded, feeling emboldened by how eager she was to have me in her mouth. She puckered her lips and applied pressure around my thickness. *Fuck me.* I didn't know how long I could last inside her before exploding.

My desire for more took over. I pulled back until just before my head escaped her lips, then rammed myself back in. I hit her deep into her throat. Her eyes widened in panic and tears escaped the corners. It was probably deeper than anything she had ever experienced before, but I knew she could take all of me with a little extra encouragement.

"Breathe, *jaan*. Relax your throat."

She exhaled forcefully out of her nose and relaxed her muscles. As soon as she recovered, I began moving in and out of her mouth. I pushed with such force that it would surely make her jaw sore later. Her hands grasped my hips for support from my abuse. More tears spilled from her eyes. Seeing her cry because of my size made my dick harden even further. I was so close to exploding.

"Make yourself cum," I grunted. She greedily slipped her hand into her yoga pants, as if she had been waiting for my order. I thrust myself relentlessly into her soft, pretty mouth. I was barely holding on.

"Get there, beautiful." She rubbed her clit furiously as I continued my assault. I felt her suck harder, and a moan escaped her throat, reverberating through my length. Her hips bucked as her orgasm pulsed through her. I followed her, feeling waves of fire fill my body as my own orgasm ripped through me.

Hot cum jetted from my head, filling her small mouth. Some of it leaked out of the corners of her mouth, dripping onto her chin.

I pulled my spent dick out of her. "Swallow."

She managed to gulp it all down in one swallow. I ran my thumb down her cheek, over her sexy freckles. My thumb collected my spilled arousal from her chin, and I shoved it into her mouth so she could suck the last bits of me off. She closed her eyes as she consumed more of me.

I came down from my high and set about fixing my clothes.

She snapped out of her daze. "Where are you going?"

"Home."

"Oh," she replied with the annoyance she'd had when I barged into her apartment.

I sighed. "Amelia, look at me." She raised her chin to look straight into my eyes. "Whatever you think this relationship is, stop. This cannot be anything more than sex."

Embarrassed that I had bluntly addressed her feelings, she shifted on the floor, casting her gaze to her hands in her lap.

I continued because I knew she was listening, "I have no plans to settle down into a long-term relationship. I respect commitment too much to sully it with my lifestyle."

She took a few seconds to process my words. "Have you ever been in a relationship?"

I didn't want to get into this, but I had promised her I'd never lie to her when she asked me a question. "Once."

Her eyebrow raised in surprise. "When?"

"A long time ago." I was barely out of high school at the time.

Amelia seemed disappointed at my revelation. "What was her name?"

"Salena."

"Did you love her?" she pressed. Her curiosity always got the best of her.

I hesitated before answering. This conversation was heading in a dangerous direction, and I should have ended it, but I continued, "I thought I could. I was engaged to her."

"Engaged?" she repeated in shock.

"It was an arranged marriage. My father wanted to strengthen our alliance with a British distributor. In exchange for loyalty, my father promised a marriage between myself and his daughter."

"What happened to her?" Her eyes were fixed on me, unblinking.

"I broke the relationship off after my father killed himself. I never wanted to get married and only agreed to because marriage alliances are necessary in our business. My parents were arranged, so I knew that feelings of affection could follow, hence why I thought I could love her. However, since my father was no longer alive, I didn't see a need to honor the contract, especially when I hadn't really wanted to settle down in the first place."

Hanging on my every word, she probed, "There must have been bad blood between you and her father after that."

"There was. He eventually started doing business with Tarun out of revenge. But I had too much respect for Salena to put her through a forced marriage."

"Do you still keep in touch with her?" Jealousy was evident in her expression.

"No. We went to Harvard together, but after I called off our marriage, she moved back home to England." Salena had understood my reasoning but had still been upset about the breakup. Because of that, we hadn't spoken since.

"Did you sleep with her?" she asked hesitantly, as if she knew I'd put my walls back up at her question.

"What did I tell you, *jaan?* Don't ask questions that you don't want answers to." I had answered all that I needed to for one day.

I left her on the floor, disheveled and with my cum smeared around her lips as I exited her front door.

XIX. Amelia

"So, have you decided what you want to do?" Nat asked as she sipped on her pumpkin-spice latte. I had confided in her the general details of my relationship with Shyam—or lack thereof.

We had finally "discussed" what *it* was. I knew I cared about him, but I didn't love him—yet. But after hearing about his stance, I couldn't help but feel hurt.

I had decided to skip my weekend tradition of camping out in my apartment and coding until morning in exchange for going shopping with Nat. I hated shopping, but I needed some dressier outfits for work. I preferred my comfortable wardrobe, but I stuck out in the sea of women with pencil skirts and black leather pumps and men with perfectly tailored suits. I didn't necessarily want to wear heels to work, but I could do with some pantsuits or even some nice blouses. Nat was a self-proclaimed expert at shopping, so she was the perfect person to help me.

"I don't know. I'm not against hooking up. I've done it before. I just thought he cared for me as much I do for him," I replied, then took a bite of my warm danish. It was one of the few fall days where the rain had held up so the sun could make an appearance, but the air still felt chilly, warning of impending winter.

I had thought for sure there was something more growing between us. But when he showed up at my place and warned me not to fall for him, my hope had deflated. He was sending me mixed messages, and I was confused.

"Guys like him are hard to read. They're used to manipulating people and situations to get what they want. It's why they're such successful businessmen," Nat said before taking another swig of her latte.

She was right. Powerful men like Shyam were used to manipulating people. They were experts at leaving people yearning for more.

"His brother said he was with a stripper the night we had sex for the first time." I had been upset when I heard that. The thought that I was getting some woman's sloppy seconds made me want to throw up. I'd wanted to give him a piece of my mind until he had stormed into my place like a raging bull.

"*Being* with a stripper doesn't necessarily mean he fucked her, right?" Nat asked.

Deep down, I didn't believe that he had slept with one either. Why would he have assured me he was clean when we had sex later that night?

"I guess. But he made it clear that he didn't want our relationship to go deeper than sex." I diverted my eyes from hers to hide my embarrassment. I felt like I was just a booty call.

"Is that necessarily a bad thing? Maybe it'll be easier for you to use him as a reference for a bigger and better job later if you stay casual. No hurt feelings in the end to complicate things?"

Too late. My feelings were hurt, and I felt rejected. He had said he didn't want to drag a woman into his unsafe lifestyle. Yet, he had been engaged to some woman, and I was only good enough for the occasional hook-up.

The way he had used me to give him head had been devoid of any emotion, but it had still turned me on. *Am I so messed up that I enjoyed the way he used me?*

He could deny his feelings for me, but he couldn't deny our chemistry. We were explosive when we were together. But Nat was onto something. Whatever happened between us, I still wanted my letter of recommendation, and maybe it *would* be easier to move on later if we just kept the relationship sexual. Getting emotionally involved with a crime lord wasn't the best move for a career-oriented woman like me.

"You have a point," I said, my head heavy with thoughts.

"Maybe you should show him what he's missing out on." Nat pulled my hand and led me to the storefront of a lingerie shop. Mannequins scantily clad in luxurious satin and lace pieces posed in the window.

I wasn't the type to wear sexy lingerie and sashay around a man for attention. I preferred my comfortable cotton bras and panties to lace.

"I dunno, Nat. You know that's not my style." I tugged on my knitted cap uncomfortably.

"Sure, it is! Don't knock it 'til you try it. I vote you wear something to make him forget about every stripper he's ever met."

Eyeing a sexy black lace bra-and-panty set with matching stockings and a garter belt was enough to convince me. I was pretty sure I'd end up in his bed again because I couldn't stay away, and I wanted to bring him to his knees. Without saying a word, I made my way to the front door of the shop and went inside.

"Hell yeah!" Nat exclaimed, pumping her fist in the air as she followed me. "I raised you well."

******

Shortly after reaching home with my shopping bags in hand, Shyam sent me a text. He wanted to have a meeting about the search with Jai and me at his weekend house. A car would arrive in one hour to drop me there.

I didn't have much time to get ready and pack my laptop bag. I eyed the shopping bags on the floor, particularly the small pink one with the fancy black calligraphy scrawled across the front.

I had just found my motivation to get ready quickly.

XX. Amelia

The car arrived right on time to pick me up. The driver helped me into the car as usual, and I settled into my seat because the drive would be a long one. I had brought my laptop for the meeting, so I could always use that for entertainment if I got bored.

I unbuttoned my coat to avoid overheating in the warm car. I had decided on a black wrap dress that showed a hint of cleavage. Underneath, I wore the lingerie set I had seen in the store window. I had never worn stockings or a garter belt. I wasn't used to this level of underwear, but the minute I put it all on and stood in front of the mirror, I felt sexy. My posture was straighter, and I liked how my body looked. I had always felt like my boobs were too small and my hips were too wide, but surprisingly, I thought I looked damn good in my new lingerie. I knew this was a business meeting with Jai in attendance, but knowing what I had on underneath gave me the courage I would need to face Shyam.

I had ended up pinning my hair up into a low bun, leaving out tendrils to frame my face. I had kept my makeup sophisticated by lining my eyes with black eyeliner and dusting my lids with taupe eyeshadow to play up my eye color. My lips were nude, but I had lined them before applying gloss to give a cleaner look.

I still had an aversion to high heels. They were pointlessly painful, in my opinion. Instead, I had opted for some black knee-high boots with three-inch heels for more support. I could still walk in them, but they gave me a little extra height, which always came in handy when facing off with such a tall and powerful man.

I was confused about my feelings for Shyam. I couldn't just turn off the part that cared for him. I understood his reasons for remaining uncommitted, but I hadn't expected him to be seeing strippers or whoever while seeing me.

That was the part that annoyed me most. He had made it sound like he wanted to whore around, but something in me knew that wasn't who he really was. I was sure he had a vivid past with women, but he had been engaged. He had probably been faithful to Salena, since he was so adamant about respecting monogamous relationships. I hadn't even considered marriage yet, let alone to Shyam, but I was jealous of what he'd had with Salena. I wondered if their sexual chemistry had been as heavy as ours.

He had put distance between us, not even kissing me after the day he had charged into my apartment. However, the fire between us was too strong to be dimmed by his control. I could see it every time he glanced at me in passing at work—the hunger and desire. Our attraction was the one thing he couldn't control, and I secretly loved that.

As the driver pulled into the garage port, I realized I had spent the entire ride mulling over our situation in my mind. I was buzzed into the elevator, and it took me to the living area. As I stepped into the space, I was greeted by Jai.

"Hey, doll. How's it going?" He kissed my cheek to greet me, like I was a member of his family.

"Hey. Not too bad." My mouth formed into a genuine smile. I had been anxious about coming back to this house, but seeing Jai eased my nerves.

"Here, let me take your coat," he said as he moved to help me slide it off my shoulders.

"Thanks," I said, pulling my arms free.

"Look at you." He took a long look at my outfit and whistled in approval. "Hot date tonight?"

I blushed, unsure of how to respond. Just then, Shyam walked into the room and approached us. He was dressed in a white button-down shirt and navy dress slacks. His tie was gone, and his top buttons were undone, showing a hint of his hard chest. He was mouth-watering perfection. His smoldering eyes took in my figure from head to toe. I felt a shiver as he inspected me. His jaw clenched as his gaze combed my body.

"She looks fiiine, doesn't she?" Jai asked, cutting through the tension that surrounded us.

Shyam didn't utter a word. Instead, he took my coat from Jai's hands and moved to the closet near the entrance to hang it up.

"Awkward," Jai sang in a low voice.

"Tell me about it," I replied. If this were any indication of how the rest of the night would go, our meeting wouldn't be very productive.

"So," Jai started. "I kind of told him that you knew about the strip club. He got all weird when I told him."

Shyam had never directly addressed the strip club the night he'd charged into my apartment, so I hadn't known that Jai had already told him. But I was starting to piece everything together. Shyam was probably pissed at Jai for saying anything to me. And from the way I had reacted, he had probably realized I had developed feelings for him.

"You!" I exclaimed while still trying to keep my voice no louder than a whisper. The last thing I needed was for Mr. Noncommittal to overhear us. "That's why he's being so cold with me!"

"Yeah, probably not the best move on my part. Sorry 'bout that." Jai grinned apologetically.

Before I could shout-whisper at Jai some more, Shyam returned to us.

"What can I get you to drink, Amelia?" he asked in his deep voice.

The way he'd said my name ignited something in my core. I raised my gaze to see his face fixed in an intense expression, like he was studying me. His words had been polite, but his eyes were expectant. My mouth suddenly felt parched.

"Uh. Water is fine. Thank you." I gave a quick and awkward smile.

He nodded and walked to the bar to get my drink. I needed my head clear around him, so alcohol wouldn't have been a good choice.

After he was out of earshot, Jai showed me to the dining table, where I assumed we would be holding our meeting. "I don't know what he said to you, but I do know that he cares about you."

I rolled my eyes. "I wouldn't be so sure of that."

"He doesn't realize it yet. In case you haven't noticed, he's a stubborn asshole," he said as he pulled out my chair. I sat down and put my bag on the floor next to me.

I tried to suppress my urge to laugh, but it just came out as a snort.

He walked to the opposite side and seated himself across from me. His laptop was already on the table, so I took mine out from my bag to set it up. Our laptops came with VPN access that was impenetrable to hackers, so it was very secure to access any data we had gathered at the lab.

"It's true. He thinks he's the most self-aware person on the planet, but he's in denial," Jai said.

"He was pretty convincing when he said that he just wanted to keep things casual." I didn't want to go into details about his brother forcing me into submission and making me suck him off in my apartment.

"I'm sure he *wants* that, but I'm not so sure that's how he truly *feels*. But he told me to mind my own business, so I'm staying out of this," he said teasingly, throwing his hands in the air in surrender.

"You have a funny way of staying out of things." I smirked. He winked back at me.

Shyam appeared at the table and placed my water in front of me.

"Thanks," I said nervously.

"You're welcome," he replied, his eyes lingering on mine for an extra moment.

He pulled out the seat to my right, at the head of the table. Sitting so close to him made me even more nervous than I had already been. *Deep breath.* I could do this. I was dressed to kill, and I wouldn't let his proximity unnerve me.

Two more buff men joined us at the table, one sitting next to me on my left and the other sitting next to Jai.

"Saran, have the new security measures been implemented successfully?" Shyam asked, starting the meeting.

The man next to me was larger than the chair that he sat in. His biceps were barely contained by his shirt and were covered in tattoos. He directed his focus toward

Shyam when he spoke. "Our most recent shipments to France and Brazil have arrived without event. We've had two men dressed as armed security guards on each shipment."

"Javed, how much are we producing per day?" Shyam focused on the man sitting next to Jai. He was just as big as Saran, but his face was fixed into a permanent scowl, making him look more menacing. I was glad there was a table separating us.

"About twenty kilos. We needed to scale back on production since sales decreased," Javed offered, his voice rough like gravel.

"How's our progress with the search?" The question was directed toward Jai and me.

Jai took the lead. "We have complete profiles on all of his men, with current photos, but no matches have come up with the facial-recognition software. They seem to be in hiding too. We've seen activity move into nearby states, as well as into Delhi. Tarun's men have set up factories in the east of Delhi." He typed busily on his keyboard as he spoke.

"That's dangerously close to our base," Shyam replied, his voice lacking any hint of surprise. The information seemed to be redundant to him. Jai had probably shared everything with him before the meeting.

I had picked up on some of India's geography since I'd started working on this project. I knew that Bengal, where Tarun was from, was on the eastern-most border of India. Delhi was in the north and held the capital of the country, New Delhi. But I wasn't sure where Shyam and Jai's Indian base was located.

I cleared my throat involuntarily as I pondered my question. Everyone turned to look at me. My cheeks flamed from the direct attention of four sets of eyes trained on me. I felt so awkward, like a kid in school getting ready to give a presentation in front of the whole class when I wasn't prepared.

I swallowed the lump in my throat before speaking. "Where is your base?" My voice sounded so small and shaky compared to the ones that came from the men who sat before me.

"Our base is in Punjab. It's on the western border," Shyam replied in his most professor-like voice. His intense gaze scorched me on contact.

"Oh." *Answer received.* I averted my eyes back to my laptop screen.

Shyam resumed speaking. I sank back into my seat as I typed out notes. Just then, a low-battery warning popped up on my screen. I had forgotten to charge my device.

I looked around for an outlet to plug my power cord into. I saw that Jai had an extension cord set up on his side of the table with his laptop connected to it. There was an extra outlet available for me. Luckily, I had packed my power cord in my bag.

Jai was responding to another one of Shyam's questions as I quietly leaned over in my chair to fish my power

153

cord out of my bag without disturbing everyone else. I felt goosebumps spread over my thighs, starting just above my knees and radiating higher up.

I looked up and found a pair familiar hazel eyes focused on my lap before they met my gaze. Shyam's expression was ravenous, like he was ready to sink his teeth into my skin to satisfy his hunger. I followed his line of view to see what had held his attention. The hem of my dress had shifted higher in my quest to find my cord. My thighs were exposed, showcasing the straps from the garter belt attached to the lace tops of my stockings. I swore I heard him growl. The sound had been low and inaudible to the others at the table, but potent enough to emit vibrations that hummed through my most private parts. My body instantly responded to his call. My pussy tingled in excitement, like it was just waiting to hear the beast before me summon it.

"What do you think, boss?" Javed's rough voice broke through the lust-filled haze surrounding us. Shyam quickly composed himself. His wall of armor went up, leaving no hint of the savage animal from seconds ago exposed. I squeezed my thighs together to ease my want, then adjusted the hem of my dress to cover my underwear and grabbed the power cord out of my bag before hastily sitting up.

"Do you need that plugged in?" Jai asked.

"Huh?" I was still shaken up from the moment I had shared with the wild man next to me. My cheeks felt flushed and my palms were sweaty.

He nodded to the cord in my hands. I looked down. "Oh. Yes, please."

I handed it over to Jai, who connected it to the extension cord and then to my laptop. I chanced a peek over at Shyam from the side and saw his face fixed into a smug expression at how flustered I was.

I needed to keep myself together. *I am the one in control.* He thought he could call all the shots between us, but I was taking back my power. Why else would I be wearing this sexy-ass lingerie, if not to bring him to his knees?

I managed my best poker face and sat up taller in my chair. Shyam continued the meeting as if nothing unusual had happened.

For the next two hours, we refined the details of our approach to the search. I would be using the photos of Vik, Tarun's brother, to find hits on any of the new photos Shyam's men captured around India. It was the only way we could locate him—by linking him to Vik's facial features.

My butt was numb from sitting with perfect posture for so long. After Shyam concluded the meeting, I packed up my laptop and cord into my bag, then excused myself to use the restroom. I needed stretch my legs and pee. The men stood up out of courtesy and continued talking amongst themselves as I walked away.

After I was finished in the bathroom, I returned to find a vacated dining room. I looked around for signs of someone in any of the other rooms, assuming the men had relocated, but came up empty.

I moved to the staircase and made my way up. Something compelled me to wander up the steps. Images of the last time I was here took over my head.

The echo of my heels clicking on the steps broke the silence around me. I found myself in front of Shyam's room. The door was closed. *Should I knock first?* My knuckles gently rapped on the wood. No answer. I waited a beat before I knocked again. Still no answer.

I cautiously pushed the door open. The room appeared to be empty, so I wandered further inside. It looked and smelled just like it had the last time I was here, when—

Shyam emerged from the closet, startling me and relieving me all at the same time. He had changed from his dress clothes to just a pair of sweatpants. The muscles on his arms and torso were tight with tension and I could see the cords protruding under his skin, like he had just been working out. He stalked closer to me, approaching slowly like an animal preparing to move in for the kill. I was his prey, frozen in my spot. His eyes were wild with dominance.

"Where did everyone go?" I managed to ask.

"I sent them away," he said as he reached me. I had barely been in the bathroom for five minutes, so it was surprising everyone had left already.

"Oh. I guess I should go, too." I said. I was about to turn on my heel to leave when he stopped me.

"Why leave so soon? Didn't you come here to tempt me? Isn't that why you came here tonight with your pretty pussy wrapped in lace, like a present waiting for me to unwrap?" The fire in his eyes burned my skin and I suddenly felt claustrophobic in my clothes. If he kept staring at me like that, I would have to rip them off to avoid suffocation. No—I couldn't give in. I had to strengthen my resolve.

Ignoring the ache between my legs, I lifted my chin higher and stared him straight in the eye. "Who says it's for you? I have plans later." I didn't, but he didn't need to know that. If we were keeping things casual, then it was none of his business. He didn't control what, or who, I did in my spare time.

His eyes widened with ferocity. I knew I had affected him with how his jaw clenched at my words. I turned and walked away, leaving him to simmer in his anger.

He pounced on me from behind, pulling my arm to spin me around into his. Strong hands gripped my body hard as his mouth crashed onto mine. I had missed the taste of his mouth, and from the way he kissed me, he had missed the taste of mine too. Lust and need consumed us both. His tongue was relentless, attempting to force me into submission. *Nice try.*

I pushed away from him. "No." I knew this game. He liked control and watching others concede to him.

"Yes." His fingertips dug into me. His lips skimmed the sensitive spot on my neck, making my belly flutter with delight. "Take off your dress so I can see what you're hiding underneath."

Strong backbone, Becker. It was difficult to resist his magnetic pull, but my heart was still wounded from his rejection. I would let him have my body, but I was keeping my heart. "You take it off."

He pulled his head back, his eyebrow raised in surprise at my command. I imagined that he wasn't used to hearing anyone tell him what to do, especially a sexual partner. He exerted pure dominance in bed, so I was certain this beast always got his way in that arena.

His lips fixed into a devious smile. His fingers traced a line from the base of my neck and down the valley between my breasts. They moved lower over my dress, until he stopped at my waist. He untied the sash that held my dress together and smoothly slid it out of the loops at the sides. My dress fell open, exposing my satin-and-lace-clad body to him.

His eyes feasted hungrily on me, and he licked his lips as he raked his gaze over my breasts. He draped the freed sash around the back of his neck, letting the tails hang loose over his chest.

His fingers skimmed over the exposed skin above the rim of my bra. My nipples hardened from his attention. He slipped his fingers under the sheer material and pinched both nipples hard. I hissed at the stinging sensation. The pain felt good. Until Shyam, I had never thought I would find pleasure in pain. But now, just the thought of it made my pussy drip with arousal.

I pulled his hands from my tits and placed them on my thighs. "Unzip my boots."

"You want control, *jaan*?" My heart melted when I heard his nickname for me. I wanted more when I heard it escape his lips. But I had to stay strong and not cave in to his charm.

He fell to his knees before unzipping each boot, painfully slow. He was teasing me. Giving up power wasn't easy for him, and he wasn't going to give it up without a fight.

I lifted my feet one at a time to let him slide my shoes off. He sat back on his heels and looked up to me. "What does my *jaan* want now?"

I was new to this too. I was used to letting the man take the lead in bed. I was so nervous, and I just prayed it wasn't showing through. I clenched my hands into fists at my sides to hold myself together.

I took a page from his book and commanded him just like he had with me when he'd stormed my apartment. "Kiss me."

He paused for a moment, probably assuming I meant something innocent, like on my mouth. I tilted my pelvis toward him to show him what I really meant. He smiled when he realized what I wanted—needed.

Fingers curled around my hips, holding me in place, he pressed his nose to the apex of my thighs, inhaling my essence as he closed his eyes. I was sure he could feel the dampness in my panties on his nose. It was as if he were savoring me. He kissed me through the fabric, and I ached for bare contact with his tongue.

He unclipped the garter straps from my stockings and pulled the belt down. Hooking his thumbs through the sides of my panties, he pulled the lacy scrap of fabric down my legs, all the way to the floor. I stepped out of the lingerie. He swiped the panties up from the floor and rubbed a finger over my arousal that had accumulated on the inside. I watched with unquenchable desire as he sucked my excitement off his finger.

"Like honey," he said without lifting his heated gaze from mine as pocketed my panties in his sweatpants. I bit my lip to suppress the moan that threatened to escape from witnessing the scene before me.

He returned his attention to my pussy, holding my hips with powerful hands. He swiped his tongue over my clit, causing my hips to buck from the contact. He gripped me harder as he continued stroking my nub with his tongue. My back arched in pleasure, giving him more access. One of his hands roamed to the small of my back, angling me onto his mouth. His tongue moved lower, to my slit. He drank from my pussy, consuming everything I gave him.

He pushed a finger between my ass cheeks. I tensed up because I knew where he was trying to go, and I had never had anyone in that area before. His tongue worked my pussy harder, making me forget about my shyness. I relaxed my muscles and let him in. The tip of his finger slid into my hole, causing my nerve endings there to explode with sensations I had never felt before.

My whole body tightened. I was at the edge. I could feel myself being pulled further into the cyclone of passion I was already lost in.

I gripped his hair with my hands so tightly that I had to have been causing him pain. He groaned at my roughness, letting me know he liked it. My whole body vibrated from the sounds he made as his lips sealed around my slit. I shattered into a million pieces, exploding as I came into his mouth. I screamed his name as waves of satisfaction overtook my body.

I held his forehead to my pelvis as I came down from my high. He leaned back when I finally relaxed my hold. Glistening with my arousal, his lips were fixed into a sexy grin. I could see his dick was ready to break free from the way it tented the front of his sweatpants, but I had found my fucking power and wasn't ready to let it go just yet.

I straightened up as well as I could, despite my legs feeling like jelly. "Lie down."

He rose to his feet, towering over me. The intensity of his hazel eyes burned brighter than I'd ever seen. For a second, I thought he would challenge me. Instead, he walked to the side of the bed and dropped his pants, freeing his erection, then lay back, with his upper back resting against the headboard.

I stood at the foot of the bed, unable to look away from the beautiful man in front of me. His tall frame covered the entire length of the bed. Ripped muscles topped with a massive, throbbing cock lay waiting for my next move.

My eyes never left his as I slipped the straps of my bra down. My hair had fallen out of its bun so I moved the tendrils over one shoulder to undo the clasp, then gently tugged my bra loose and dropped it onto the floor, leaving myself stark naked except for the stockings on my legs. I placed a knee on the bed and crawled over the man waiting for me. I was on all fours over his body when my face met his. I licked my lips, eyeing his bottom lip, then placed a kiss on him. Our mouths started to move in unison—licking, sucking, devouring.

He broke our kiss, panting with need. He was the picture of composure in public, but in bed, he was wild and untamed. I knew it would ruin me in the end, but I had to attempt to tame the beast before me. I noticed the sash from my dress still around his neck. I tugged on one end to free it.

His lips spread into a sly smile. "What is my *jaan* planning to do with that?"

I stared at him without giving away my thoughts. "Are you afraid?"

He answered with a question of his own. "Should I be?"

"Yes," I replied after a beat.

His smile grew wider. He offered me his hands, crossed at the wrists. "I should have you know that I'm usually the one tying people up."

"You've never had anyone do this to you before?" I thought I knew the answer, but I wanted to hear him say it. When this relationship was over, I wanted him to remember me for something that he had never experienced before. He had, without a doubt, fucked a lot of women, but he *would* remember me.

"No," he answered in his deep voice.

I smirked, enjoying his answer. "Good. I like a virgin."

He chuckled at my witty retort. I wrapped one end of the fabric around his wrists, tying a knot around them.

"There's a hook behind the headboard," he said.

I looked at him in confusion. His eyes darted to the other tail of the sash to show me what he meant. He hadn't been kidding about being the one who tied lovers up. Jealousy shot through me at the evidence before me. I grabbed the sash with more force than necessary, pulling abruptly on his wrists, then looped the fabric through the hook and tied another knot. My breasts rubbed against his face in the process. I sat back, admiring my work—his arms over his head, leaving him fully at my mercy. I loved this feeling of having total control over him.

"Do you have any condoms?" I asked. I assumed he kept a store of them in his nightstand drawer.

He looked at me with annoyance. "No. I need to feel you."

"You're the one who said this wasn't a commitment. I'm not going bare if you've been with other women. Like strippers." I couldn't help but add that last jab. I was illogically immature when it came to the idea of him with other women.

"Trust me, I'm clean," he said.

"How can you know that?" I argued.

"Because I just do."

Unhappy with his answer, I remained stubborn. "I'm using protection, even if you are clean. I don't trust your whores."

He sighed with frustration at my snide remarks. "Amelia, there hasn't been anyone else since you."

"Oh," I replied quietly at his admission. I had assumed he was seeing other women after he'd demanded that things remain casual between us. I had thought for sure he had slept with that stripper.

Emboldened by the power I held, I lowered myself onto his bare cock. My pussy felt tight as I made my way down his length. I moved slowly to give my walls a chance to stretch to his size. I finally reached the base, and all the discomfort I had felt was replaced by the urge to move.

I slid up and down, my cream coating his shaft. The lubrication allowed me to move faster. My tits bounced in his face as I worked him harder. He moved his hips up to meet me, giving me more friction when my clit rubbed against his skin.

"*Jaan*, I need you to get there. I can't hold on any longer," he grunted through clenched teeth. Sweat dotted his brow.

My leg muscles burned from exertion, but I couldn't stop. Hearing his need to release only pushed me harder. My belly muscles tightened as I chased my own release.

My body tensed up as I rode Shyam harder. "Shyam," I screamed. Suddenly, like a dam releasing water, I came as pleasure rushed through me.

He pounded into me harder as I rode the waves of my climax. "Amelia," he shouted as he filled my pussy with hot cum.

I collapsed onto his chest out of exhaustion. My body stilled as I listened to his heartbeat slow to a steady pace. The rise and fall of his chest as his breathing relaxed soothed me.

Something was missing—I longed for him to hold me against his body. Then I remembered he was still tied up, and I rose to my knees and undid the restraints. As he rubbed his wrists together to massage them out, I noticed the ring he always wore. I had seen it a few times before, as well as on Jai, but had never asked about it.

"Do you always wear that ring?" I asked.

"Yes," he answered lazily, tired from all that we had just done.

"Why?"

He took it off and handed it to me. It was heavy, solid metal. The silver material shone in my hands. I slipped it onto my thumb, but it still was loose.

"It's our family ring. Jai has one, too. All dealer families in India have one."

I studied the design on the face of it—a snake in the shape of an "S," with black diamonds for eyes. "What does the snake mean?"

"It's a king cobra, our family crest," he replied as his fingers stroked the skin on my thighs.

"Does that mean Tarun has one?"

"Yes, his is made of yellow gold, with a Bengal tiger on it."

I knew his headquarters was in Bengal. "Because his base is in Bengal. Makes sense. What's the significance of the cobra?"

He had softened inside me, but I didn't want to move just yet. I felt our juices leaking out of my pussy and coating his skin as I continued to straddle him.

"Everyone thinks that to be the best, you have to be the biggest and most obvious predator. The cobra may be small, but it is adaptable to any situation. It hides where

166

you least expect it and strikes without warning. The venom is so fatal that it can take down a grown man with one bite."

My thoughts wandered to how dangerous this man was. Often, when I was so wrapped up in our intimacy like when he kissed me or shared stories about his family, I forgot that he was a killer.

I couldn't think of a better way to phrase my next question. It was probably better to just bluntly ask it. "Do you enjoy killing people?"

He considered it for a beat before responding. "Would it scare you if I said I did?"

Yes. He had warned me that he was a monster. I shouldn't have been taken aback by his response. He had given me fair warning. I knew what he did and how he did it. Nevertheless, I was still stunned. I didn't think a person could ever get used to hearing that their lover enjoyed killing people.

I shifted on top of him out of unease. His dick hardened under me again. He got off on my fear.

He rolled me over, pinning me to the bed. His eyes were full of intensity. The ring was still hanging loosely on my thumb. "I warned you, *jaan*. I'm not the good guy. I'm the snake who'll bite you when you're not looking." He nipped at my neck. I yelped at the sting.

He pushed himself back into me, pumping with quick strokes. I gasped with need.

"Are you my mongoose?" he groaned.

"What?" I managed to ask between breaths.

"The one animal who can kill the cobra. Will you be the death of me, *jaan*?" He deepened his angle into my pussy, hitting me at that perfect spot that made my toes curl. This man knew my body so well.

"What if I just want to tame the snake?" I moaned.

"You can try, my little mongoose. But you could also get yourself killed in the process."

Heat spread between my legs at his threat of danger. He rode me with such force that I was blinded by ecstasy. We found our release in unison. I lay under him, my arms clinging around his neck and my body spent.

"My sweet mongoose, we're far from done for the night." A mischievous smile spread across his face as he slithered down my body for more.

XXI. Amelia

I had been working non-stop all morning manually configuring altered images of the photos that Jai had shown me of Vik. Hopefully, one of these would match up with any suspected photos of Tarun that the men might capture. I was putting all my hopes on the possibility that some similarity between the two brothers would trigger a match. I hoped I was right. It was a long shot, but I didn't have much to go on without any current photos of Tarun. I would have to just pray it worked.

I looked at the time. It was nearly noon. I sat back in my chair and stretched my arms overhead. My muscles were sore from the weekend—deliciously sore. Shyam had worked me relentlessly all night and into the early morning hours. He dropped me home afterward, and I had spent the next day in bed catching up on sleep and resting my body.

It had felt good to dominate him in bed for a change, even though the night had ended with him taking over. I loved commanding him and seeing how eager he was to please me. That was probably how he felt when he had me at his mercy.

I had gained more confidence in the bedroom. Nat used to call me a prude because I would cringe every time she shared stories of her sexual escapades. I hadn't thought I would have the courage to ask for what I wanted in bed, let alone tie up one of the world's most powerful drug dealers and ride him until I came around his dick. My pussy walls clenched just reliving the memory.

I stood up from my chair and decided to grab lunch. I had chosen one of my new outfits today—a charcoal-gray pencil skirt, a black blouse with slightly puffed sleeves, and coordinating cable-stitched tights. I had added some black chunky-heeled loafers for comfort.

Maybe I'd eat outside today. The weather seemed fair, slightly overcast and chilly, but no rain. I grabbed a throw blanket from my sitting area and headed downstairs to one of the lower-level cafeterias. The kitchen near my office was amazing and the staff was more than accommodating, but I wanted to enjoy my lunch in a more low-key environment—though, granted, the entire building was fancy. I just wanted to grab a tray and eat outside like a regular employee at Sethi Tech.

The cafeteria was busy since it was rush hour. The food here was still classier than anything I had gotten used to eating at my old job. I grabbed a plate of spaghetti Bolognese and a bottle of sparkling water. I eyed the elaborate pastry counter, with its rows of decadent desserts. My mouth watered at the sight of the chocolate mousse torte. I asked the lady behind the counter for a slice and loaded it onto my nearly full tray.

The air outside was crisp and heavy. Snow would be making its first appearance of the season soon. I could feel it.

The deck was serene, despite nearly all the tables being occupied by employees. There was a fire pit in the center of the deck that gave the area a cozy feel, and the view was astonishing. I could see the tops of tall skyscrapers looming overhead. In the distance, I could hear the faint honking of car horns, but I was so high up that it wasn't disturbing at all.

I found the last vacant table and set my tray down. Draping my throw blanket around my shoulders, I slipped out of my shoes and curled up cross-legged in my chair under the warmth of the fabric.

I took a bite of my pasta. Steam wafted from my plate, mixing with the cold, ambient air. I closed my eyes, savoring the tangy and meaty flavors. Nothing beat comfort food on a cold day.

A man's voice interrupted my food-gasm. "Hey, Amelia."

It was Blake from the financial department, tray in hand. He had helped me set up the stock options I'd received when I was hired. *Yes, Amelia Becker had stock options!* Most of the employees were offered them as a benefit of working for the company. It wasn't an extravagant amount, but it was a nice bundle that I could leave to earn some interest. Maybe I could use it to buy Mom a new house someday.

"Oh. Hi, Blake," I replied, trying to swallow my pasta so I wouldn't seem like a pig talking with my mouth full.

Blake was tall and easy on the eyes. He looked like an Abercrombie model with blond hair and classic good looks, especially in his cardigan, light-blue dress shirt, and tan slacks. He looked like he had been a surfer before he relocated to the city.

"You seem really into your pasta. I kind of wish I got that instead of this sandwich." He looked down at the baguette sandwich on his tray in mock disappointment.

I giggled. "Whatever...that looks amazing too!"

He grinned. "Nothing compared to comfort food like pasta on a cold day, though."

"I completely agree!" I smiled at how coincidental his comment was.

"Well, I just wanted to say hi. I'll see ya around," he said, turning away to look for an empty table, but he was out of luck. He turned back to me. "I guess everyone else had the same idea before me."

"Want to join me?" I asked, pointing to the empty chair in front of me.

"You sure you don't mind?"

"Not at all." I really didn't mind the company. I hadn't made any new friends since I had been at Sethi Tech, so I welcomed new conversation.

Setting his tray down, he asked, "Do you eat out here a lot?" He took a bite of his sandwich.

"No, this is the first time I've been to this cafeteria."

"I bet the dining room is amazing on the top floor," he said, wiping the corners of his mouth.

"I'm afraid I haven't used that either. I tend to just eat lunch in my office." I usually got so carried away with my work that I didn't want to leave and interrupt my train of thought.

"That's a shame. This building is like a luxury hotel. You should take advantage of the perks."

I shrugged. "I guess I'm just used to quick lunches from my old company."

"Where'd you used to work?" he asked with genuine interest.

"IP Innovations. It was a startup, but Sethi Tech acquired it," I replied, taking a sip of my water.

"Yeah, that happens a lot when Sethi Tech is involved." He took another bite of his sandwich.

"How about you? How long have you been working here?"

He put his sandwich down and wiped his hands on his napkin. "About two years. I used to live in Huntington Beach before I moved here."

"Let me guess—you used to be a surfer?" I took a bite of my torte and moaned at how luscious it tasted on my tongue.

He stared at my mouth as I took another bite from my fork. Clearing his throat, he replied awkwardly, "Um. Yeah. How'd you know?" He directed his eyes away from me and back onto his plate.

I knew it! He was a California boy. "Just a hunch. What made you move all the way out here?"

"College," he said.

"Me too. Where did you graduate from?"

"NYU."

"Oh, really? I did too!" It always excited me when I met someone from my university. I knew the odds were high, since it wasn't far, but it was still exciting.

"I wonder if we ever crossed paths there. Were you in any sororities?" he asked, excited by the coincidence too.

I nearly choked on my water. "Me? Sorority? No way."

"Not a fan of Greek life?" He smirked.

"No, nothing like that. I was just kind of a loner. I guess I still kind of am." I redirected my gaze to my plate. I felt awkward discussing my lack of social depth.

"That's why you're a prodigy."

I looked up to see an expression of genuine kindness on his face. Confused by his answer, I asked, "What?"

"Come on. You don't think people talk? You're young and beautiful, so naturally, people are interested in you."

I was shy at the idea of people talking about me behind my back. I knew I stood out from the typical Sethi Tech employee, but I guess I hadn't realized how noticeable I was.

"Don't worry," he continued. "People only ever have good things to say about you. You don't seem to be the typical snobby upper-management type that they normally hire. You come off as a genuine hard worker."

I felt relieved hearing that. I *was* a hard worker, and I didn't want anything to tarnish that reputation. "That's good to hear. I still feel a little out of place here. I usually find it difficult to meet new friends."

"I'm not so sure of that. You seem perfectly comfortable making new friends." He offered me an encouraging smile that lit up his whole face, then scrunched his napkin up before placing it on his tray.

It felt good to have a new friend.

XXII. Shyam

Jai must have been able to tell by my tone that it was important and that I needed him as soon as possible, because he came within five minutes of my text— a rarity.

"What's wrong?" he said as he rushed into the lab. He found me staring at one of the computer screens. He pulled up a chair to see what held my attention.

Salena. She was dressed in the finest dark-pink and gold fabrics, like she was getting married. I had seen her dressed like this once before, at my side. Her *lengha*, or skirt, shone with jewels and beads in intricate designs. Her *choli,* or blouse, matched her skirt, but it fit so loosely on her frame. Salena had always had a curvy frame, with full breasts and ample hips. But in this photo, she was as thin as a rail. Her eyes were sunken in like she was under stress and hadn't slept well. Her fair skin, which she had inherited from her mother, was bruised with black marks that looked fresh, like she had just been through a fight. A *dupatta,* or veil, covered her head in the traditional way that brides wore it, but it couldn't hide her expression—or lack thereof. Her eyes were vacant. She looked like a corpse propped up to pose for a photo.

I looked down to her hands and saw that they were adorned with traditional henna and glittering gold bangles. The vibrancy of her adornments made her skin look even paler.

I noticed something odd as I looked closer. She wore gold handcuffs in addition to her bangles, a chain connecting the cuffs. They were the most elaborate and expensive handcuffs I had ever seen.

"What the fuck happened to Salena? What is this?" Jai asked, enraged. He had been close to her when we were engaged, so I knew seeing her like this upset him just as much as it upset me.

"This was sent to my email address. Read the file name."

He read the title. "'Salena and Tarun—Engagement.'"

My jaw clenched tighter hearing him read it aloud.

He looked up at me in confusion, as if he had read a foreign language that he didn't understand. "How did this happen?" he asked.

"He's going after everything that was once mine." Tarun wanted to prove a point with what appeared to be a forced engagement with my ex-fiancée. Salena looked anything but consenting. I found it hard to believe that her father had let this happen, but then again, he wasn't against giving his daughter away if it meant filling his pockets with money. *Piece of shit*.

"Let me see if I can find the IP address from where it was originally sent," Jai said as he took control of the mouse and keyboard. He clicked on a tab and typed something into the search field.

"Well?" My patience was waning.

His eyes flicked back and forth as he read the data he needed on the monitor. "The IP address is showing that it was sent by your computer in your office."

I shook my head, truly perplexed. "That's impossible. No one has access to my computer except for you."

"Whoever sent it probably altered the address and used yours to throw us off. Hackers do it all the time to get through firewalls."

"What about the coordinates of where it was taken?" If we could get the coordinates, then we could move men to scour that location.

His fingers flew across the keys again. "Dammit. It's encrypted," Jai exclaimed as he banged on the keyboard.

Of course, it was encrypted. If this had been sent by Tarun or his men, they wouldn't have made it easy for us to solve. They liked working in riddles.

"Can you decrypt it?" I asked.

"Yes, but it could take weeks. Tarun has a good tech team behind him, so I'm sure this won't be easy to crack."

"We don't have that kind of time. We need to locate this asshole now. He's fucked with us one too many times." I clenched my hands into fists, trying to contain my frustration. When I was frustrated, I punched shit.

"He probably used a newer and more complex method of encryption to encode the coordinates, but decryption that way can take a long time if we're trying to hack the location," Jai said.

I didn't know much about encryption techniques. My technical knowledge was limited. I relied on Jai to fill in the gaps for me. "How sure are you that he's used this type of encryption?"

"Fairly certain. It's the most common method people use these days because of its level of security." Jai clicked the mouse a few more times and opened a new program. After inputting some information, a status bar appeared, signaling that something was being processed.

"There. I've set up the decryption cycle. The system will alert our phones to let us know if coordinates were decoded."

"What if this doesn't work?" I asked.

"It's very possible that it will not. This type of encryption is difficult to hack. The program will either just keep running in a loop and never end or it will error out when it exhausts all of the possible combinations of bits to make up the coordinates."

I stared at the picture. My ex-fiancée sat in front of a window that overlooked lots of tropical green trees. She could have been anywhere in India from the setting in the background. Nothing specific stood out to me about her location.

She looked so broken—a shell of the woman she had once been. I hadn't spoken to her in years, but I still felt protective of her. I cared about her and didn't want her to be the subject of Tarun's abuse because of his vendetta with me. She deserved better than this fate. She'd had a free spirit when I knew her, and to see her like this was difficult. She was just another casualty of this business, a game piece used by the men who controlled the board.

Jai's voice interrupted my thoughts. "I downloaded the photo to the cloud so that Amelia can access it too."

Dread filled my gut. What if Amelia was next? Her vacation request had just been approved for Thanksgiving next week. She was taking a week off to fly back to Seattle.

What if Tarun tried to take her while she was away? She had no idea how much danger she was in. If something happened to her, I wouldn't be able to live with myself.

Tarun would stop at nothing to take whatever was mine. And Amelia was *mine*.

XXIII. Amelia

My vacation request had been canceled! *What the fuck?!* I was supposed to be flying out to Seattle this weekend to spend the week with my mom for Thanksgiving. I had already booked my tickets and started packing.

I was stunned as I sat staring at the email from HR saying that my once-approved request had been "canceled due to increased staffing demand." *What does that even mean?!* It was Thanksgiving week! What could possibly be so important that they would need staff in the office?

I didn't even really work for the company. My job had nothing to do with anything related to keeping it running smoothly. This had Shyam written all over it, and I was enraged.

I marched down to his office and demanded his secretary let me see him. She said that he was in a board meeting. I was more irritated that I couldn't storm into his office and tear into him immediately like I wanted to. His secretary asked if I wanted to leave a message, but I spun away, too enraged to reply to her. It was rude, but I wouldn't have been able to form a coherent sentence anyway.

I stalked down the hall to the group of conference rooms where I knew he held his meetings. Only one room had a "RESERVED" sign on the digital monitor outside of the door. The privacy blinds had been drawn, so I figured that was the room that he was in.

I put my hand on the doorknob, and for a moment, a sliver of clarity broke through. *This is way too dramatic, Becker.* The good angel on my shoulder was probably right. But the bad angel on the other was fucking pissed at being bossed around by a control freak. I turned the knob and pushed into the room.

Eight men in perfectly tailored suits and with leather portfolios and fancy fountain pens on the table in front of them drew their attention toward me. *Shit. Maybe I should have listened to that good angel.*

I knew all the men sitting in the room because we had offices on the same floor, and I had seen them in passing. They stared at me with confusion and interest.

Jai was seated at the far end of the table. Judging from his expression, he was trying to suppress a laugh. He knew who I was looking for and was totally here for the show about to take place.

Shyam sat at the head of the table, glaring at me. He did not find my intrusion as amusing as Jai did. I stood my ground and faced off with him wordlessly, glaring back with such fire in my eyes that he finally rose to his feet and pressed his knuckles into the table before him.

"Leave." His voice was low but full of venom. No one questioned him, or even spoke. They left their belongings behind and filed out of the room in silence.

Jai remained seated and crossed his ankle over his knee, getting ready for the drama about to unfold before him.

"Get the fuck out," Shyam growled at his brother without even looking in his direction.

"Shit. I never get to stay for the fun," Jai joked as he strolled toward the door.

He stopped to nudge me playfully with his elbow on the way out and whispered, "Godspeed." He closed the door behind himself.

I started before Shyam had a chance to talk. "Who the fuck do you think you are?"

He raised his eyebrow at my choice of words. I rarely ever cursed aloud, so I was sure he was surprised by what had come out of my mouth.

"Your boss," he replied, asserting his dominance over me. "Care to explain to me why you interrupted my meeting?"

"You had HR cancel my vacation!" I said, pointing an accusatory finger at him.

"What makes you think I had anything to do with it?" His voice remained steady, unlike mine.

I threw my hands in the air in exasperation. "Why else would they approve it and then deny it?"

"I need you to work next week."

"Over Thanksgiving? That's bullshit," I snapped, resting my hands on my hips as I waited for a better response.

Trying to distract me from the purpose of my tirade, he said, "That mouth of yours has certainly become dirty, hasn't it?"

I ignored him and pressed on. "I had plans! My mom is expecting me. I already booked my tickets."

"Cancel them. She'll understand," he said as if it were no big deal. Maybe it wasn't to him, but my mom was important to me.

"No! Practically the entire company is on vacation next week, except for me? That's not fair!"

"I will not be on vacation. I will be working too." He probably never took a vacation. I couldn't imagine him snapping pictures on the streets of Rome with gelato in hand like a tourist.

"Shyam, I miss my mom. I want to see her. Why are you doing this?" I pleaded.

He stayed quiet, deep in his own thoughts. He was hiding something from me.

I walked around the table to where he stood. "Hey," I said gently as I put my hand on his bicep. He turned his face to look me in my eyes. "Talk to me."

He let out a huge sigh. "Salena is engaged to Tarun."

"What? How do you know?" I knew he didn't talk to her anymore, so I was confused about how he'd know that. Was he bothered that Tarun was involved or that his ex-fiancée was taken?

"Someone sent an untraceable photo of her in engagement clothes," he said, sounding almost detached.

"Was Tarun in the photo?"

"No."

"Were you able to figure out where it was taken?" Maybe it had coordinates associated with it that we could use to find Tarun through her.

"No, the coordinates were encrypted. Jai is running software to decrypt it right now," he said.

"That could take weeks or even months to figure out," I said, thinking aloud.

He grunted in frustration. "If we can even decrypt it at all."

"What does this have to do with me leaving?" I still didn't see how this affected my trip home.

"Amelia, she had bruises. She didn't look like herself. She's being held prisoner." His eyes were filled with worry.

This was worse than I'd thought. "She's being forced to marry him?"

"I'm sure of it. He's trying to prove a point, taking everything that I've ever had."

I didn't want to be presumptuous, especially after he had blatantly told me how he viewed our relationship, but I itched to ask what was on my mind. "Is that why you don't want me to leave?"

He didn't say anything, but concern showed heavy in his eyes.

My heart softened at his silent admission. He was worried about my safety. He wasn't one for many words when it came to his feelings, so I didn't expect him to say anything in this moment.

I moved into his body and wrapped my arms around his waist.

"I promise, nothing will happen. I'm taking a direct flight to and from Seattle and going straight to my mom's house when I get there. I promise to check in with you every day."

He embraced me back, holding my hips with his hands. "No going anywhere alone. Understand?" he ordered.

"I promise," I said as I rested my cheek on his chest. He relaxed a little and his chin rested on top of my head, encasing me in his warmth. "You have to trust me with information that you know, Shyam. I'm in this fight, too."

"I know," he said, holding me tighter.

Now, I wasn't so sure I wanted to leave him for a whole week. There was no place safer than in his arms.

XXIV. Amelia

Seeing my mom again after so long was amazing, but it also made me feel sad. The resemblance between us had always been remarkable, especially with our matching red hair. Except now, she looked older and more tired. It broke my heart that she was working so hard and lived alone all the way out here.

We spent hours catching up and reliving old memories. I missed her so much. She had been such a devoted mother when I was a child. The relationship had changed as I got older and we had become friends. I could trust her with anything.

Thanksgiving was a small affair in our home. It was just Mom and me, so we cooked just enough for two people. Instead of a huge turkey, we opted for a couple of small Cornish hens, cornbread, roasted vegetables, and mashed potatoes with gravy—because who didn't love mashed potatoes?

I was by no means a great cook like my mom, but I could hold my own in the kitchen. I was busy prepping the vegetables for the oven while Mom was making the marinade for the hens. We, of course, indulged ourselves in a few glasses of wine while we cooked and chatted.

"So, have you met anyone special in New York?" she asked as she worked.

I hesitated at her question, unsure of how to answer. I wasn't sure if I was ready to share the news of my complicated relationship with Shyam. I was usually honest with her and valued her advice when it came to guys, but Shyam wasn't like the others—definitely not the type you'd bring home to meet your mom.

I decided to rip the bandage off and tell her. She'd know if I was lying anyway.

"Kind of," I replied without looking up from my cutting board.

She set down her bottle of olive oil and clasped her hands in front of her chest. "Oh! That's wonderful, sweetheart! How long have you been together?"

"Just a few months." Things had escalated quickly in the few short weeks that I had known him.

"And I'm just hearing about this now?" She sounded a little offended that I'd kept the news from her.

"I'm not so sure he's the right person for me." I kept my gaze low to avoid eye contact with the woman who could read me like a book.

Concern washed over her face. "Why do you say that?"

I didn't know what to say. I couldn't tell her about his criminal activities or the real reason he had hired me to work at Sethi Tech. I would have to just give her a condensed version of the story.

"He's just…intense." Or maybe just the ultra-condensed version.

"What does that mean?" she asked in confusion.

"It means he's not like the other guys I've dated." *Definitely not like the other guys.*

"Let me guess—he's a 'bad boy'?" My mom had always been a sharp lady.

I smiled at her guess, and she knew she was right.

"You get that from me. I was always falling for the bad boys when I was in my prime."

"Mom, you're still in your prime."

"That's sweet of you to say, but you know what I mean. Does he treat you well?" I knew my well-being was most important to her.

He did. He was always honest with me and made me feel special when we were together. Even though he was unable to commit, I knew he cared for me. He had proven that to me when he'd tried to sabotage my vacation.

I had texted him every day while I was here, as promised, and although he still seemed cranky about me leaving, he always replied with short messages of confirmation shortly after receiving my texts. If I was being honest, I missed him. It was weird being away from him.

"He does. He's just not looking to be in a committed relationship right now," I said, organizing the vegetables on a baking tray.

"And what do you want?" She resumed streaming olive oil into her bowl of chopped herbs and spices.

"Me? I guess I thought we'd be something a little more than casual by now."

"Sometimes these bad boys take a little more time to realize what they want. Your dad did," she said, too busy to look up from her marinade.

"Huh?" This was news to me. I hadn't realized my dad had been a bad boy afraid of commitment. He had always seemed strongly devoted to my mom when he was alive.

"Your dad was so afraid of commitment when I met him. He was always faithful to me, but he was still hesitant to settle down."

"I had no idea! How did he end up changing his mind?" I abandoned my vegetables, needing to hear more.

"I gave him space and time. He came around at his own pace. The important thing is that you continue to live your life while he figures out what he wants. You're a bright young girl. Don't get caught up in others' indecisiveness. Experience life instead of waiting for someone to commit to you."

"So, you're saying I should date around in the meantime?" I didn't want to see other people.

"Only if that's what you want to do. I'm not saying you should be one of those crazy loose girls." She waved her hands in the air like she was a college girl on spring break.

"Mom!"

"You know what I mean. You have integrity and you should hold onto that. But if you want to see other people, that's fine too. These guys sometimes need a little space to realize what they're missing out on."

"You're right mom." She always was.

"What's his name?" She cocked an eyebrow as she dug for more information. Moms always needed to know more.

"Shyam," I said.

"That sounds like an Indian name."

"It is. He and his brother Jai are from India."

"Are his parents still in India?" She tasted her marinade and added more salt to season it.

"No, they passed away a few years ago," I replied, depositing my tray into the oven and setting the timer.

Her face turned somber. She knew about loss. I did too. "That's a shame. He must be lonely."

"I guess he is." I knew he was. It was why he was so guarded with his feelings.

"How did you meet?" She coated her hens with the dressing she'd prepared, using a brush to keep her hands clean.

"Well, he's my boss." I turned away to pretend to check the oven even though the vegetables had barely been in there for a few minutes. I didn't want to see her expression.

"Amelia Becker!" she scolded playfully, pinning her hands to her hips.

"He bought over IP Innovations and hired me to work for his company," I argued defensively.

"You don't have to defend yourself to me, honey. I know you're brilliant. He is lucky to have you as an employee."

"He agrees with you and treats me like I'm smart. He believes in my abilities as a programmer." He believed in me even when I doubted my own abilities.

"That's good. I should be warning you not to let a man with power take you for granted, but I know I raised an independent girl. You learned from my mistakes." Her voice was heavy with regret.

"Mom…you were a great mother, and it wasn't your fault that Dad died." I came to her side to wrap an arm around her shoulders.

"Yes, but I wasn't as independent as I could have been, so I wasn't prepared for his death. It took me a while to get back on my feet."

"But look at you now. You're providing for yourself and you raised me after he died. I'm so proud of you, Mom."

"Thank you, sweetie. That really means a lot to me." She kissed my cheek. "So…when do I get to meet him?" She took another sip of her wine and played coy.

I smirked. "I don't think introducing him to my mom when he wants a casual relationship is the best idea."

She laughed. "Maybe not. But I'd love to meet him, whenever you're ready."

******

Despite our small meal, we managed to stuff ourselves until we couldn't eat anymore. We spent the rest of the evening watching old black-and-white movies that Mom loved and talking until we couldn't keep our eyes open.

I had just showered and changed into a pair of shorts and a tank top to get ready for bed. My hair was still wet from my shower, so I left it loose to dry a little more before sleeping.

I leaned back on my bed, propped up by pillows, and scrolled through my phone to catch up on social media.

My room was like a time capsule of my teen years. Star Wars posters decorated the walls. I still had glow-in-the-dark stars stuck to the ceiling. I had also had a weird obsession with lava lamps at one point, so I had them in various sizes and colors on my desk at the far end of the room. I had been such a sci-fi fan growing up, and I loved anything that reminded me of outer space or computers.

I had received a few missed texts from friends wishing me *Happy Thanksgiving* throughout the day. I even had one from my new friend, Blake.

Happy Thanksgiving, Amelia. Hope Seattle is treating you well. Let's get together when you get back.

It felt nice having a friend at work. Whenever we crossed paths, we always chatted, but we had never met outside of work. It would be fun to get to know him better. I thought he'd really get along with Nat and my old IP Innovations friends too.

I texted everyone back. I hadn't heard from Shyam, so I decided I should wish him *Happy Thanksgiving* too. I didn't know what traditions the Sethi brothers had for holidays, but I was guessing it didn't involve a nice meal in a dining room and arguing over football. I couldn't imagine Shyam carving a turkey or Jai passing around stuffing.

Instead of texting, I hit the phone icon on my screen. The phone rang once before he answered.

"*Jaan.*" That one word in his familiar voice made my belly flutter with excitement.

My nerves got the best of me; I didn't know how to respond. "Hey."

"Are you okay?" he asked. He was still on edge about Tarun.

"I'm fine. I just wanted to wish you a Happy Thanksgiving."

He chuckled. "It's not Thanksgiving anymore."

I suddenly realized the time difference. He was three hours ahead, so it was after midnight there. "Oh, I'm sorry! I forgot how late it was there. Were you sleeping?"

"There's no rest for the wicked." And he certainly was wicked.

"Did you do anything special...yesterday?" I asked.

"Like eat turkey? No, I was working." No surprise there.

"You didn't at least get together with Jai?"

"Why would I? He was out whoring around. Probably still is." I was glad it was just Jai who was whoring around the city this evening.

"Maybe he needed a wingman?" I teased.

"I think we both know he needs no help in that department."

"True."

The line went quiet for some time.

He spoke first. "How are things at home?"

"Great. I love being home with my mom."

"She must have missed you a lot." He seemed genuinely interested in hearing about my time at home.

"She did. I wish she lived closer, so I could see her more often." I couldn't hide the emotion in my voice.

"Maybe one day you can move her out to the city."

"Or maybe I could move back home." There were plenty of amazing tech jobs in Seattle.

The line was thick with silent tension. "Are you considering moving back?"

"I'm not sure. I won't really be needed after we...um...accomplish what we need to." I didn't want to say too much over the phone. Shyam had taught me that ears were listening everywhere, even where you wouldn't suspect them.

"There are plenty of jobs available in New York for you, especially with the letter of recommendation that you want from me. You would no doubt secure these jobs without my help, but the letter would be a bonus." He sounded like he was trying to convince me to stay.

"I don't know that there'd be any purpose for me to stay in New York." I wanted him to beg me to stay because he wanted me to.

He took a long sigh. "There'll always be a purpose for you, *jaan*."

I was hoping he meant it in the way that I wanted.

After another long silence, he spoke. "It's late. You should get some rest."

"Yeah, it is. Well...good night." I wasn't ready to hang up yet. I wanted so much to tell him that I missed him, but I didn't want to risk getting rejected again.

"Good night."

"Shyam, wait!" I called out hastily before he could hang up.

"Yes, *jaan*?"

I paused for way too long. "Never mind."

He hesitated before speaking, as if considering how best to respond. "Me too."

He knew exactly what I wanted to say.

XXV. Amelia

The rest of my vacation passed by quickly. Mom and I decided to play tourists in the Seattle rain and do some sightseeing. It was so much fun getting to experience my hometown this way with my mother. We took goofy photos at the Space Needle and bought *pirozhkis* at Pike Place Market.

Now, it was time for me to head back to New York, and my heart felt heavy leaving her again.

"Mom, I'm going to miss you so much," I said as I hugged her goodbye outside the security line at the airport.

"Sweetie, you have no idea how much I'll miss you," she replied through her tears, squeezing me tight.

I pulled back so I could look at her face one last time. "I hate the idea of leaving you here."

"I'll be fine. I will come visit as soon as I get some time off from work." She rubbed my shoulders reassuringly.

"I would love that, Mommy."

"You take care of yourself. I know I don't need to worry about my good girl too much."

"One day, we'll live together again so we can be close together," I promised.

"You're a young, vibrant lady. Why would you want to live with an old bag like me?"

"Because I love you," I said, squeezing her tighter.

"I love you, too. But you need to enjoy your twenties. You need to experience life on your own. It's all part of growing up. I will always be with you, no matter where you are," she said, pointing to my heart.

I started crying again as I held her one last time before heading into the line.

*****

It was a long flight. I kept tearing up for the first half hour, before eventually falling asleep. I slept the rest of the way until we reached the gate. I looked like a hot mess in my over-sized NASA sweatshirt, jeggings, and sneakers.

I grabbed my roller bag from the overhead compartment and deboarded the plane. I didn't have any check-in luggage, so I walked past the carousels as I went through baggage claim.

It was dark outside already, so I decided to stop and pull out my phone to check on my Uber before exiting the airport. My driver was close, so I headed through the doors to wait on the curb until the car arrived.

I noticed a black Ferrari parked by the curb with a familiar man leaning against the passenger-side door with his hands in his pockets.

Shyam came to pick me up at the airport? He hadn't let me leave in the first place without having my flight itinerary, but he hadn't mentioned anything about coming to get me.

I stood there with my mouth agape and my eyes wide with shock.

He was so sexy in those dark jeans and a black t-shirt. He looked like he hadn't shaved for the day, and all the stubble only made him look more rugged and handsome.

The corners of his mouth lifted into a grin when he saw me, and I was a goner.

I forgot about my bag and threw myself into his arms. He held me as people bustled past us to find their rides. It was so noisy but, in that moment, I couldn't hear anything except for the sound of his heart beating inside of his chest as I pressed into him. I savored his warmth and smell—leather and tobacco.

He pressed a kiss to the top of my head before I broke our embrace. "How long were you waiting here for?"

"Not long. I checked your flight status before driving over." He grabbed my bag and loaded it into the trunk before opening the passenger door for me. I scooted in and secured my seatbelt as he made his way to the driver's seat.

He sat inside and turned towards me. Gently taking my face in his hands, he stared at me like he was memorizing every detail. His fingers caressed my under-eyes, knowing that I had been crying. He pressed his lips to the delicate skin under each one.

I closed my eyes, enjoying the feeling of his lips touching me. His kisses made their way down my cheek and to the corner of my mouth. My breath faltered with anticipation. I longed for his lips on mine. As if sharing the same feeling, he took my mouth.

Our kiss started out slow, as if he wanted to take his time with me. I parted my lips, inviting him inside. Taking advantage of my summons, his tongue invaded me. I kissed him back feverishly, tangling my tongue with his. I felt our souls unite and erase the time that we had been apart.

He broke our union, leaving me panting for air—or maybe just for more of him.

"You've been crying," he said, ignoring the cars honking impatiently around us.

"It's always hard to leave Mom," I said.

He shifted gears and pulled away from the curb. "You should have her visit."

"I think I will." I smiled.

We drove off into the night, the engine roaring as we went. His hand rested on the gearshift as he drove. I had spent a week away from his touch, and I didn't want to be away from it anymore. I slid my hand over and linked my fingers with his, my palm on the back of his hand. He turned his hand over and grabbed mine so that our palms were facing each other, fingers intertwined.

Instead of pulling up to my building, we pulled up to a lavish apartment building that looked like a five-star hotel from the outside. Shyam helped me out of the car and grabbed my bag. A valet took the keys and tended to the car.

I followed Shyam into the building, and the doorman greeted us with a courteous smile on his face. "Good evening, Mr. Sethi."

"Good evening, Henry," Shyam replied to the bald middle-aged man.

The lobby was gorgeous, with marble floors and huge flower arrangements on pedestal vases around the space.

"Where are we?" I asked.

"My home in the city," he replied, unaffected by the grandeur around us as he ushered me to the elevator. He was probably accustomed to it, since he saw it often.

We rode the elevator all the way to the penthouse suite.

The space looked like his house—decorated with sleek furniture in masculine tones. A fire roared in the fireplace. Huge windows overlooked the city, providing the most beautiful soft lighting in the background.

Shyam left my bag by the couch and pulled on my hand firmly, leading me into the bedroom. The walls were dark and only a small bedside lamp illuminated the room.

As soon as we were inside, his hands grasped either side of my face and pulled me to him for a scorching kiss. He massaged my tongue with his, using slow, meaningful strokes. My hands moved to his chest, clutching his shirt.

He undressed me, lifting my sweatshirt over my head and pulling my jeggings down to free my legs. I kicked off my shoes to make it easier to step out of my pants.

I lifted his shirt up and he helped me pull it off. I worked on his jeans, discarding them onto the floor in the growing heap of clothes. He pulled off his boxers, revealing his fat cock. My eyes dilated in arousal. I removed my bra and panties, leaving myself fully naked in front of the tanned god before me.

Shyam stared at me with a look of hunger that I had never seen before. He backed me up until the backs of my knees hit the bed. Pushing us onto the mattress, he lay over me and rested his hardness on my belly. Precum wet my skin on contact. We kissed until we needed to catch our breaths.

Warm, wet lips skimmed down my neck. I felt his tongue lick at my skin as they ventured lower. He palmed my tits—squeezing them, rubbing them. His teeth found my nipple and clamped down onto it, causing sparks of pain and pleasure to radiate through my chest and down to my pussy.

I hooked my legs around his back and pressed my pelvis up, begging him to enter me. This time, he didn't make me wait.

He separated my pussy lips with his fingers and shoved himself into me. "Fuck. I missed this," he grunted as he pushed himself all the way in, hitting my cervix. He wanted his dick to touch all of me. He pumped into me, propping himself up with his palms grasping my tits.

His strokes were slower than usual, causing him to have more contact with my walls than when we had fucked hard and fast in the past. This wasn't fucking. This was something else.

I felt myself teetering on my edge. He leaned in closer to me, with his mouth hovering just above my lips. Our breaths blew onto each other's faces. I dug my fingers into his hair and pulled his mouth over mine, kissing him as I gripped his dick with my pussy.

I felt my muscles bear down on his shaft. Orgasm hit me, causing moans to rip from my throat. "Babe," I shouted as I came harder than I ever had before.

The fire in his eyes burned bright hearing the endearment that had slipped out of my mouth. I'd thought it would scare him off, but instead, he pumped harder into me. His body shook as he exploded inside me, spilling his warm cum into my slit. He groaned as he filled me until our juices leaked down my ass.

He adjusted himself on top of me, with his forearm resting on the mattress above my head to keep from crushing me under his big frame. His nose nuzzled the side of my neck as we caught our breaths. My fingers pressed into his back, holding him close to me.

He rolled onto his back and stared up at the ceiling, giving his body a chance to body recover.

I turned my head to look at him in the dark. "I'm sorry. I didn't mean to say that."

He didn't look upset or withdrawn. "I liked it."

"You did?" I asked in surprise. "I know *this* isn't something serious between us, but it just came out."

"*Jaan,* I said I liked it," he said gently to get me to stop justifying it. After a beat, he asked, "Do you want to go home tonight?"

I don't. "What do you want, Shyam?" The ball was in his court now.

"I'd rather you stay," he said unapologetically.

Closing the distance between us, I snuggled into his side. "Then I'll stay."

XXVI. Amelia

Christmastime was my favorite time of the year. The air was light with cheer and the decorations always made me smile.

When I'd lived at home, my parents would take me to the tree farm so we could cut down our own tree and make the house smell woodsy, like a pine forest. I would always choose the burliest and most rounded tree. My mom would make an event out of it, dressing us up in red plaid shirts and rainboots. We would always sit near the firepit at the farm and sip some hot cocoa after strapping our tree to the top of the car.

Holiday festivities in the city were certainly different than in the Pacific Northwest. The decorations here were more elaborate and extravagant. The stores were decked out like Christmas playgrounds for the masses. It was a whole new level of holiday for me, and I loved it.

Nat and I decided to invite Blake to take part in our holiday excitement at the tree lighting in Rockefeller Center. It was my second year in attendance, and this year seemed more packed than the last, but we didn't mind the crowds. It just added to the merriment.

I was bundled up in a red chunky-knit sweater and jeans paired with comfy over-the-knee boots as I waited in line for hot cocoa. I shoved my hands into my coat pockets even though they were covered by gloves because it was really cold out. I was glad I had remembered to put on my knitted cap for extra warmth.

I made my way back to my friends while trying to balance three steaming cups of cocoa in two hands. Blake came to my aid, grabbing two cups from me.

"Thanks, Amelia," he said. He looked handsome in his black coat and jeans, with a charcoal scarf around his neck. He passed a cup to Nat.

"I fucking love cocoa!" she said as she warmed her hands around her cup. She had opted to be themed out instead of warm, wearing a dark-red corduroy skirt with leggings underneath and a white peacoat. Her bright-orange hair was styled into braids on either side of her head. She looked like a badass elf.

"Do you know how to ice skate?" Blake asked us.

"I do!" I shouted over the loud noise from the crowd surrounding us. I loved ice skating. I wasn't amazing, but I could stay upright for more than a minute.

"Oh, hell no! I'm not going to bust my ass on that ice!" Nat exclaimed dramatically.

"You're just scared to ruin your outfit when you crash," I teased. Blake chuckled.

"Whatever. Don't hate because you ain't great," she said, flashing us her middle finger, indifferent to any children who might have been watching.

"Come on!" Blake took my cup and set it down next to his. Grabbing my hand, he pulled me toward the rink. I turned back as he dragged me along and waved to Nat apologetically for abandoning her.

After renting our skates, we stepped onto the ice. The rink was full of different levels of skaters. The more seasoned ones zoomed past us. Blake seemed to be steadier on his feet than I was.

"Do you skate a lot?" I asked.
"I took lessons when I was a kid." He crossed one foot over the other, following the curviest edge of the rink.

"Skating lessons in California?"

"Hockey," he said as he glided gracefully alongside me.

"Still...in California?" I reiterated.

"I know it doesn't seem like the type of place for winter sports, but we had a rink near my house."

"Isn't hockey kind of...violent?" I asked, putting my arms out for extra balance.

"Not *kind of*. It's very violent. But I was young when I played, so we weren't trying to prove our manliness by beating the crap out of each other yet." He flashed me a grin that lit up his handsome face.

His smile was infectious, and I returned the sentiment. "You seem to be really athletic."

"Yeah, being active is a huge stress reliever for me, especially since I have a nine-to-five job. It helps doing something active after work to release all the tension from the day. What about you? Play any sports growing up?" he asked.

"Ummm, not really. I was too obsessed with computers to leave my room. But since I lived in the Northwest, my parents forced me outdoors. They'd make me hike with them sometimes or go kayaking in the summer. They were big into camping too." Although I knew my way around a computer better than the average person, I could also fish, start a fire from sticks, and pitch a tent. I didn't like doing those things, but my parents had made me learn so I could help while we camped.

"That sounds peaceful." He turned so he was facing me, skating backward.

"I used to hate it, but now I miss it." I would have given anything to go back to the days when I had lived at home and my dad had still been alive.

I was too wrapped up in our conversation to notice a large nick in the ice in front of me. The front of my skate caught in the hole, causing me to tumble down to the ice. Blake tried to catch my hand on the way down, but I pulled him down with me.

He landed on top of me, his firm arms encasing me on the ice. His eyes caught mine as we lay there amidst the other skaters zooming around us. His expression turned serious as his gaze drifted toward my lips. *Oh no.*

I cleared my throat to dissolve the silence between us and turned my face away from his as I tried to push up to stand. He quickly righted himself first and then extended his hand to offer me help. I accepted his assistance and got up as quickly as I could.

"I'm such a klutz," I said, nervously laughing off the whole thing.

Blake followed my lead, downplaying my rejection. "Are you okay?"

"Yeah, I'm good. Just more embarrassed than anything," I said as I ran my fingers through my hair to hide any evidence of my fall.

"At least you're a graceful faller." His smile didn't reach his eyes like it normally did. This was just a polite smile.

I chuckled. "You're too kind, but thanks!"

We made our way out of the rink and pretended our almost *whatever* on the ice had never happened. We found Nat stuffing her mouth with a warm cinnamon bun. She had frosting smeared on the sides of her mouth.

"Hey!" she said with her mouth full.

"Hey," Blake and I answered in unison.

"How was the rink?"

"Great," I said, adding a "Where'd you get that from?" to get her to change the topic.

211

"The booth at the far end. I would have gotten you all one, but I didn't know how long you'd be skating for. It tastes so good warm!"

"Oooh, I'm going to go grab one," I said, hoping to put some space between myself and my *friend* who almost kissed me.

"Allow me," Blake said, sounding as eager as I was to get away.

"Oh, thanks." I smiled.

"No problem. I could go for one too," he said, then he rushed off in search of treats.

I sat next to Nat on the bench to rest my ankles.

"Your boyfriend is going to be sooo pissed!" she sang as she rocked her shoulders side to side, dancing to her little song.

"Who?" I asked. "Shyam?"

"Do you have more than one now? Oh wait, I think you just might!" she teased. *Ugh, she saw us.*

"I don't have any boyfriends." Shyam and I were a lot closer lately, but I still wouldn't label him as my *boyfriend*, especially since he had made his feelings clear about it in the past.

"I'm guessing your 'revenge lingerie' didn't work?" She took another huge bite of her bun.

"He liked it, and that's all I'm sharing with you about that." I really didn't want to share the details of how I had tied him up and fucked his brains out. Although, thinking about it right now made my inner-most muscles clench.

"Then he won't mind that you're hanging out with Blake tonight? You know...since he's not your boyfriend."

Shyam was possessive over me. He had nearly beat the shit out of his brother when he'd caught us alone on my first day at Sethi Tech. I was sure he wouldn't be too thrilled with me hanging out alone with Blake.

But I wasn't alone. We were in a group, and it was purely platonic—at least on my part. I wasn't going to tell him about my awkward moment with Blake on the ice, especially since we weren't exclusive. I didn't owe him an explanation. It would just be too much drama about nothing.

"No, not at all," I lied.

"Good to know," she said, cocking an eyebrow as a sly smile spread across her lips.

XXVII. Shyam

"How many possible combinations of bits have we cycled through to decrypt the coordinates?"

"Nearly half a million. And no matches yet." Jai leaned back into the couch in my office.

I leaned against the fireplace mantle, with a migraine spreading over my skull.

"Fuck." I rubbed my eyes in frustration. We had had no luck decrypting the coordinates from the picture of Salena yet.

"This could very well take weeks longer to decrypt. Or it could fail altogether," Jai said.

"There has to be a match. We'll just have to keep trying." We needed to get to Tarun to save our business and free Salena. She didn't deserve to be caught up in any of this because the men in her life had decided to live the way they did. She was innocent in all of this.

I scrolled through my phone to check my messages for any updates from my men back in India. I saw a missed message from a number I didn't recognize.

Hey, just wanted to invite you to a party for our fave girl! Amelia's birthday is next Saturday, so let's meet up at Giovanni's at 8 p.m. And remember, it's a surprise, so don't say anything to her! XoXo

"Who the fuck is this?" I said aloud. Obviously, it was one of Amelia's friends, but I didn't know much about her personal life, so I couldn't name any of them. I had seen some of them when I'd interviewed everyone at IP Innovations, and in passing at Nirvana.

"What?" Jai asked, looking up from his own phone.

"Amelia's birthday is next week and one of her friends texted me an invite. I have no clue who it is."

"Ohhh, yeah, I got that text too. It's one of her IP Innovations friends, Natalie. The one with the orange hair."

I recalled the girl he was talking about. She had also been at the club with Amelia when I had first had her to myself. How did Jai know who she was? He had interacted with her even less than I had.

"How did you get an invite?" I asked.

"I guess I'm one of Amelia's *friends*, too." He smirked.

I wanted to be with her on her birthday, but the idea of a party with tons of jabbering girls made my migraine worse. I preferred to get her alone and do filthy things to her twenty-four-year-old body.

I'd thought I couldn't get enough of her before, but after being apart from her for a week while she was in Seattle, my hunger had increased. I had missed her presence. I had been in a bad mood all week waiting for her to come back to me.

I knew she could have found her way home from the airport, but I couldn't have waited another minute to see her. My thoughts strayed to her often throughout my day, but when she went back to Seattle, I couldn't get her out of my head. I kept wondering what she was doing and if she was safe. I longed for her sweet smell in my bed and her delicate touch on my skin.

She was the best lay I'd had. She made me feel like a fucking king every time she came around my dick and screamed my name. The other night when she called me *babe,* she made me come harder than I had ever come in my life. I thought my chest was going to explode from how fast my heart raced during my release.

When she told me that she wanted to move back to Seattle, I saw red. I knew I'd have to let her go eventually after we finished our mission, but a pit formed in my stomach just thinking about it.

If being away from her for only a week had driven me nuts, I couldn't imagine how letting her go for good would make me feel. She was brilliant and beautiful and deserved to spend the rest of her life with a safe and well-providing man—and I would still want to tear that man up alive, even though he would be better for her than I was.

Now that she was back, I wanted her all to myself and didn't want to share her attention. But I supposed it was selfish of me to expect her to spend her birthday with just me.

"Well, are you going?" Jai asked.

"And let you spend her birthday with her while I do all the work?" I caved and did something selfless for once. "Yes, I'll go."

"Great. I'll sign your name on the card. You bring the balloon bouquet," my pain-in-the-ass little brother teased.

XXVIII. Amelia

Nat said she was taking me out for my birthday. We were going out to dinner at my favorite Italian restaurant and then out for dancing and drinks.

I assumed it would just be the two of us because I didn't know who else would be able to come out for my birthday during the holidays. People were probably busy on weekends doing their Christmas shopping or making plans to fly home to visit family.

I knew Blake was still in town, but we hadn't spoken much since our awkward night at the tree lighting. Still, I was completely okay celebrating with my best friend. We always had a great time together.

Twenty-four wasn't a milestone age, but I still wanted to look nice for the evening. Nat set up an appointment for me to have my hair and makeup done. I opted for a look that was more daring than I was used to.

The stylist was a very fabulous man who was overly excited to style my unruly red hair. It was straightened and styled into a high ponytail that sat at the top of my head—a clean and sleek look. My eyes were smokey and topped with chunky glitter shadow. My cheeks were contoured, drawing attention to my cheekbones. Bubblegum-pink gloss made my lips appear pouty and full.

Nat and I had gone shopping for outfits too, and I had fallen in love with a silver-sequined dress with thin straps. The neckline hung low on my chest, showing off my cleavage. It showed off my legs and much of my back. It was skimpier than what I was used to wearing, but I figured it was my birthday, so I should live a little.

Lately, I had become more comfortable with my body and didn't feel as shy about wearing things that were more risqué. I still hated heels, though, even though Nat had insisted I wear shiny, strappy ones to match my dress. *She better hold my hand while I walk, so I don't nosedive into the pavement.*

We entered the restaurant and checked in our coats. We followed the hostess to what I thought would be our table, but she kept walking to the back of the restaurant, to a private dining room. I followed Nat inside.

"Surprise!" I clutched my heart and jumped back in surprise, nearly falling over in my heels. Nat proved good on her word and saved me from my fall. The room was full of my friends, who lined the far wall under a huge "Happy Birthday" banner overhead. My old friends from IP Innovations were all there. I was happy to see Blake there too, even though we hadn't cleared the air yet.

I looked at the group of people smiling and singing to me and noticed even Jai had made it. I supposed we had become friends over the past few weeks, and I genuinely enjoyed his company, even though I was technically his employee.

Continuing down the line, my eyes found those deep hazel ones that I had seen so many times. Shyam was there. He stood on the end next to his brother, with his hands in his pockets. His mouth fixed into a soft smile when I noticed him. I was touched that he had come out to celebrate with me. I hadn't even told him it was my birthday.

I completely forgot about the rest of the people and could only focus on the devilishly handsome man across the room.

Nat grabbed my arm and ushered me to the table. "Come on, girl. Let's sit!" She directed me to the seat in the middle.

"Wow, guys! I had no idea! Thank you so much!" I said as I sat down.

"The look on your face was hilarious," said Blake as he took the seat to the right of me.

Nat moved around the table and sat across from me. "Yeah, you looked scared shitless."

Jai took the seat next to her and chuckled. "I was thinking I'd have to drive you to the hospital for a heart attack or something."

Large hands pulled out the chair to my left. Shyam sat down silently, his tall frame barely contained by the chair. Everyone at the table chattered amongst themselves as they looked at the menus to scope out what they wanted to order.

"Thanks for coming," I said in a low voice, warm with gratitude. I knew that this kind of group setting was probably not his idea of a good time.

He leaned in closer to me, enveloping me in his dark, manly scent. "Happy birthday, *jaan*."

My smile grew wider.

"I'm not so sure of you looking this sexy out in public where everyone can see what's mine." His words spread goosebumps over my skin.

I blushed at his possessive intent. "Don't worry, no one is looking except for you," I flirted back.

"What were you thinking of ordering?" Blake turned to me, oblivious to our conversation. Shyam didn't appreciate the interruption and glared at Blake like he was about to strangle him, but he was a big boy and could deal with me receiving attention from my friends on my own birthday.

"Hmmm, it's between the risotto and the gnocchi. They're both sooo good," I replied as I examined my menu.

"How about I get the gnocchi, you get the risotto, and we share?" he asked, leaning in closer to look at my menu. He looked handsome in his sports coat, white t-shirt, and jeans—like an all-American hunk. He had a sweet personality to match. He would make some girl lucky one day, just not *this* girl.

I folded my menu closed and placed it on the table. "Oh, I couldn't ask you to do that." I was glad things weren't awkward anymore, but I didn't want to lead him on either.

"No, really. I don't mind," he insisted.

I could feel Shyam fuming next to me at our exchange. His jaw was tight, and I could tell he was probably clenching his fists in his lap. I had never told him about Blake because we didn't really share conversations about my friends. He had never discussed any of his friends with me either, but something told me he didn't have many.

I looked up and noticed Nat was scoping out the scene playing out in front of her. Her eyebrow was cocked high and an amused smirk had spread across her face. She was loving the drama.

I decided it was probably just easier to give in to Blake instead of argue, since he wasn't good at taking a hint. I would at least get my two favorite dishes out of it. "Okay, sounds good."

The waiter came to bring us bottles of wine, or scotch, in the case of Shyam and Jai. He took our orders and cleared the menus before leaving us to our conversations.

"You look beautiful tonight," Blake said, once again directing his attention to me.

My cheeks turned red and I awkwardly tucked an imaginary strand of hair behind my ear out of habit. "Um...thanks."

I couldn't bear to glance at Shyam's face because I knew he was livid. I looked at Nat, and she had her palm pressed to her mouth tightly to suppress her laugh. I needed to remember to kick her ass later for getting me into this predicament in the first place.

Other than the soap opera happening around me, I was having a great time at my party. The conversation and wine flowed freely. Jai seemed really wrapped up in his conversation with Nat. Who would have thought they would have hit it off?! Everyone seemed to be getting along, except Shyam and Blake.

I had always felt alone since moving out to the city, but it was wonderful to know that these people had taken time out of their schedules to be here to celebrate with me.

The waiter returned with our food. "Here, take some gnocchi," Blake said as he spooned some onto a spare plate for me.

"Thanks," I said. I did the same with the risotto and passed it to him.

I took a bite of my risotto and closed my eyes, indulging in its richness. I let out a quiet moan as it melted on my tongue. I opened my eyes to find Blake staring at my mouth. I knew Shyam was looking, too, because I could feel the heat of his gaze on me. *Shit.* I'd thought I was being quiet, but I guess I was wrong.

"That good?" Blake asked.

"Mmmmhmmm," I managed to murmur with my mouth full.

"You have a little bit of risotto here," he motioned to the side of my lip.

I moved to wipe it off with my napkin, but Blake beat me to it, using the side of his thumb to remove it.

By now, even Jai was staring at the awkward love triangle. He was loving this just as much as Nat because he knew how pissed his brother was.

"Uh, thanks," I said, dropping my napkin back into my lap. I chanced a peek over at the brooding man next to me. He calmly sipped his scotch and was even engaged in conversation with my friend Dave from my old job. He couldn't disguise the fury in his eyes from me, though.

I continued to eat my food in silence, when I felt a hand from my left slide under my napkin and rest on my bare thigh underneath. I looked over to where the hand had come from and saw Shyam still engaged in conversation. I looked at my plate to keep from drawing attention to us.

His fingers stroked my skin, creeping higher under my dress. My breath hitched as he marked his territory. He wanted to remind me of who I belonged to.

The backs of his fingers rubbed against the front of my thong over my clit. I knew I was already dripping from the feel of my underwear against me.

My breathing picked up, and I was afraid of anyone noticing. I grabbed my wine glass and pressed it to my lips to hide the breaths that escaped from my nose.

His fingers rubbed against me faster. My body grew hot with need and sweat beaded over my skin. Nobody, not even Blake, could see his hand working me, since the napkin was large and took up my entire lap. If anyone looked at us, they would just think Shyam was sitting rather close to me, but that would be it. His arm was still since his wrist and fingers did all of the work.

I felt myself edge closer to my sweet release, just before those thick fingers pulled away from between my legs. An involuntary squeak of frustration escaped from me as I moved the glass of wine away from my lips.

"Are you okay?" Blake asked with concern.

I quickly nodded and filled my mouth with wine so I couldn't reply to him. I knew my voice would give away the state of the rest of my body.

I swallowed and looked over at Shyam. He had never even stopped his conversation. *That bastard is too good.*

*****

The rest of the evening continued with good food and lots of cake. Nat thought it was funny to shove some

225

cake in my face when I was cutting it. I laughed so hard, licking frosting off my hands and mouth. Everyone else had a good laugh, too.

Shyam never touched me again but continued to keep tabs on Blake with frequent side glances. I prayed Blake didn't do anything else to set Shyam off again. My body couldn't take any more punishment.

We cleared out of the restaurant. My hands were full of gift bags, flowers, and even a balloon that Jai had brought for me. We made our way into the cold night. It was too late to hit up the club, and I was ready to head home and finish off what Shyam had cruelly started, with my vibrator—alone.

Everyone kissed me goodbye and gave me more well wishes before going on their way.

Jai pulled me in for a hug. "Happy birthday, love."

"Thanks for coming." I hugged him back. I was so appreciative that he had come. I had a great and easy relationship with him, like he was an older brother. It was nice to see him outside of work.

Nat hugged me next. "Happy birthday, bitch," she said as she smacked my ass. *Always endearingly inappropriate.*

"Thank you so much for everything, Nat. It was the perfect birthday!"

"No problem, babe. You deserve it."

"By the way, remind me to thank you personally for *everything*." She knew what I meant.

"Looks like this saga is just getting started." She tilted her head in the direction of the two men who stood in silence waiting for my attention. "Fill me in on what happens next."

"Where are you going?" I asked.

"I'm giving her a ride home," Jai interrupted. He had a stupidly excited grin on his face.

"Hmmm." I eyed them suspiciously. "Don't do anything I wouldn't do," I warned him playfully.

"I should be warning you of that. Seems like your night is going to be double the fun." He winked at me.

Two guys at once is not my thing. I could barely handle one at a time.

Jai walked over to his brother and patted him on the back, saying his goodbyes.

Blake came over to me next. "Need any help with those?"

"No, I'm okay," I said.

"I'll walk you home," he offered.

Shyam approached us before I could answer. He grabbed the gifts from my hands and made his way to the car that sat at the curb. Opening the door, he commanded, "Let's go."

I couldn't believe he had just been so rude, like a dog marking his territory. I was so embarrassed.

I looked at Blake apologetically. He seemed disappointed, and I felt bad that he had the wrong idea about us. I knew he had been trying to hit on me all night, and I was hoping he'd taken my hints. But I still felt bad about rejecting him.

"Well, enjoy the rest of your birthday," he said, resigned.

"I'll call you..."

"Yeah, sure," he said as he turned and walked away alone.

I turned back to Shyam, who had given the driver my gifts to put in the trunk. I was angry at him for being a jerk to Blake. Even though the guy couldn't take the hint that I wasn't interested, Shyam had been out of line with the way he'd acted. I glared at him.

"Get inside, Amelia. It's cold," he barked at me.

"You don't get to tell me what to do. You were so rude to my friend." I crossed my arms over my chest, standing my ground.

"Friend? He wanted to throw you on the table and fuck you in the middle of dinner." His voice grew louder. Anyone walking by could hear us.

"You're being dramatic. He just has a crush on me. It's harmless."

"Guys aren't as innocent as you think. I know what they're thinking. And it's more devious than your innocent mind can imagine."

"Not all guys are horny cave men like you," I shot back, putting my hands on my hips.

"*Jaan*, they are. Now, get in the car before I put you inside myself." He totally would, too.

I stomped my way to the car and got inside. I'd be damned if he was going to manhandle me in public.

"Take me home," I said as he slid into the car.

"I'll take you wherever I want to." He really was infuriating.

I turned my body to face the window as we rode in silence. We pulled up to his penthouse in the city. At least we hadn't gone to his weekend house, or I'd have had to sit in the car next to him, stewing in my anger, for even longer.

I rushed to open the door myself and jumped out before he could come around to help me. I left my presents in the trunk, too annoyed to retrieve them.

He yanked my arm like a child and dragged me through the lobby. There were a few people who stood back, gawking in silence. This was in stark contrast to the last time I had visited this place, when he had been so gentle and loving with me. This time, he dragged me all the way to the elevators.

The doors opened to his penthouse. I marched into the living room, even madder than I had been before, and threw my clutch and coat on the floor. "I'm not a fucking child. You can't treat me like that in public."

"Are you embarrassed that your little boyfriend got his feelings hurt?" He stalked up to me, invading my personal space.

"I don't have a boyfriend. *You* made sure of that." My words had dual meanings, referring not only to Blake.

His eyebrows furrowed with annoyance. He threw me over his shoulder barbarically and stormed upstairs to his room.

I flailed my arms and legs to get free, hitting his back with my fists. "Put me down." My dress rode up my ass, flashing his face.

He smacked my ass hard. "Shut up."

He threw me down hard onto the bed. I scrambled to get away, but he grabbed me before I could set my feet on the floor and pushed me back down. He pulled off his belt and wrapped it around his hands a few times, looking like the picture of dominance. His pupils were dilated with desire, while his cock was straining against his pants to be freed. This turned him on—having me at his mercy.

He grabbed my wrists and tied them together, wrapping the end of the belt around them. He yanked hard on his knot so that the leather cut into my flesh, then flipped me over onto my stomach and tied the other end of the belt to the base of the headboard—so that I stayed flat on my belly.

I pulled on the restraint and couldn't break loose. "Let me go!" I yelled.

"Not until you learn that you are mine."

I heard clothing drop to the floor behind me. The mattress dipped under me, and I felt the heat from his body on the backs of my thighs. He yanked on my hips, causing my ass to rise as I rested on my knees for support. My ass was on full display for him.

My breasts pushed into the mattress since I didn't have my arms to prop myself up. I turned my face to the side so I could see what he was doing behind me. He pushed the hem of my dress up higher, to my waist, and forced my thong down my thighs. I shivered as I felt cool air skim over my wet folds. Strong hands kneaded my fleshy cheeks. My breathing was out of control.

"So perfect." His warm tongue licked at my slit, tasting me. I moaned at the contact. He moved lower to my clit and massaged it. My body responded instantly, tensing as it chased its climax. He continued to work me, sending me screaming as I fell over the edge.

Before I had a chance to recover, he slammed his cock into my me. I was still so sensitive from my release, and the feeling was too much for me to handle. He pumped hard into me, slapping his balls against my clit.

"I can't," I pleaded with him to give me a break.

He pulled out of me.

"Thank you," I panted, grateful for his mercy.

I felt fingers return to my slit. He smeared my cream upward, to my hole. He massaged around my crack and slipped a finger inside. I knew what he was planning. "No, I've never done that before."

"Relax, *jaan.*" He kneaded my cheeks to get me to obey him.

His dick was so big, I knew it couldn't fit inside of me. My ass was virginal. I had never done anal before and had never had the desire to. I had heard stories about how much it hurt.

"Please, don't," I begged again.

He kissed my ass cheeks gently and fondled my nub with his fingers. I got lost in pleasure again, feeling myself near orgasm once more.

Without warning, he pushed the tip of his cock into my ass. It burned. I was too small. He was too big. It was all too much.

"Do you trust me, Amelia?" he asked.

I would always trust him, even if I thought he was a jerk at times. He had never misled me before, and I knew in my heart he wouldn't do it now.

"Yes," I whispered.

He pushed harder. I was so tight that I thought my muscles would push him back out. He remained slow and steady, feeding me more of his fat cock. He groaned when he was finally balls deep, then halted to give me a moment to adjust to his size.

He started to slowly move, rocking into me. My muscles relaxed a little more with each stroke, and the burn slowly turned into something different—yearning.

He picked up his pace as I loosened around him. His hand snaked around to my clit, rubbing circles to give me the friction I desperately needed.

I was losing my mind with the sensations I felt.

He slammed into me hard, making my hips jerk forward from the force. "Who owns this ass?"

I couldn't form words; all I could do was feel.

He yanked on my ponytail, pulling my head back. "Say it. Who owns this sweet fucking ass?"

"You do!" I screamed.

"Remember that from now on. This. Ass. Is. Mine." He pumped into me so hard that I thought I would split in half.

233

"Please," I begged again—and not for him to stop.

He slipped two fingers into my pussy as he continued his assault on my ass. I felt so full.

"Fuck," I screamed, feeling my orgasm within reach. His cock stiffened inside me.

"Babe," I cried out again as he pushed me over the edge, sending me exploding like fireworks.

He followed me, shooting his hot seed into my ass. We collapsed onto the bed together. I lay flat on the bed, with my legs wide and his dick still in me. I could feel his heart pounding against my back.

When we caught our breaths, he pulled out of me and untied my hands. My wrists had red marks from the belt cutting into my skin. He grabbed them and rubbed them out, kissing each of them to ease the burn.

He held my face in his hands and pressed soft kisses to my lips, so different from how he had just treated me. "Are you okay?"

I nodded.

"Did it hurt?"

"A little. But it felt better than I thought it would." I hadn't thought I would ever enjoy anal, but I had.

He got out of the bed and went into the bathroom, probably to clean up. He returned minutes later and took my hand. He led me to the tub, where he had prepared a bubble bath for me.

He climbed in and helped me inside. My ass felt sore as I dipped into the water. I lay on him with my back against his chest.

"The bath will help with the soreness," he said as he pulled my hair loose from the hair-tie I wore.

With the gentlest hands, he set to cleaning me with a washcloth. When he was this considerate and soft with me, he made my heart feel things.

"I like it when you're this gentle with me," I admitted with my eyes closed, enjoying the tenderness.

"You don't like it when I'm rough with you?" I could hear the smirk in his voice.

"I do, but this soft side of you is different and I don't see it often."

He let out a sigh. "I'm not a gentle man, Amelia. But you make me go from raging mad to calmer than I've ever been with no warning."

"You don't need to worry about Blake. I'm not interested in him." I sighed, relaxing into the warm water.

"I know you aren't. But I don't trust him. You are mine," he said firmly, as if to remind me of his ownership.

"You can't expect him to know that when we keep our relationship quiet," I said, my tone serious.

He considered my words. "You know my reasons for that. However, I am only seeing you. And I expect the same from you."

I understood why he didn't want to commit. It still hurt deep down, but his reasons were honorable. I was okay with this type of monogamy for the time being. "I know. I'll talk to him."

The water grew cold, so we got out and wrapped ourselves in warm towels. He left the bathroom to dry off and change. I stayed to wash my face and brush out my wet hair. He had left one of his t-shirts on the counter for me. I pulled it over my nakedness. It was way too big on me, but the material was soft and smelled like him.

He was already in bed when I returned to the bedroom, the covers drawn up to his waist. His broad chest was bare as he lay back, checking his phone. I moved to the other side of the bed.

A small red box sat on the pillow. My eyes flashed back to Shyam in question.

"Happy birthday," he said, smiling as he set his phone down on the side table.

I picked it up and pulled off the lid. Inside was a large pendant—a cobra. It was made of white gold and looked like it was slithering upward in the box, just like the one on his ring. Diamonds glittered along its body. It hung on a delicate white-gold chain. The eyes were made of black diamonds. It was such a beautiful piece of art.

He took the box from my hands, pulled out the necklace, and unhooked the clasp. I sat on the bed and pulled my hair to the side so he could put it around my neck.

"Only Jai and I have rings bearing our family crest. But you're an important part of our team now. You are one of us."

I really was. My vendetta against Tarun felt personal. Anyone who hurt Shyam, hurt me. And I wanted revenge, too.

I turned to him and clutched the pendant in my hand. "We'll find him. I promise."

He moved closer to me, appreciation for my sincerity shining in his eyes. "I know."

He kissed me softly, giving me everything I would ever need from a man. We thanked each other using our mouths. I thanked him for being in my life, and he thanked me for sticking this through with him.

We spent the next hours enjoying each other's bodies. He took his time with me, since I was sore from earlier. He slowed everything down, just like I had told him I liked, showing how much he appreciated me, until we fell asleep in each other's arms.

After a few hours of sleep, the first few hints of morning light shone through the window. I was curled into Shyam's side, with my leg hiked over his body. I lazily opened my eyes and watched his beautiful face as he slept. He was so relaxed and beautiful—at peace. His hair was mussed from my fingers grabbing it all night long. All the intensity from his face was gone. His breathing was slow and steady.

My heart felt full when I was with this man. I couldn't imagine ever leaving him. When we parted ways after completing this mission, I would miss him with all my heart. Things had changed between us.

I felt for the necklace he had given me. My teammate. My partner. This gift would always be a reminder of what we had once meant to each other, long after we were over.

XXIX. Amelia

It was the night of the Sethi Tech Annual Holiday Party. The lobby of the building had been transformed into a magnificent banquet hall with fine linens and waitstaff who greeted employees with trays of champagne and hors d'oeuvres. Live jazz music played on a stage at the center of the space. The giant Christmas tree that had been erected for the season glittered with hundreds of twinkle lights, setting the mood for a beautifully festive event.

All employees were welcome to attend—everyone from janitors to the most-senior board members. It was the Sethi brothers' way of thanking their staff for working hard all year. Everyone looked fantastic and more relaxed than during work hours. Laughter and small talk filled the room over the music. The vibe was carefree and cheerful.

I had decided on a sleeveless gown that skimmed the floor. It had looked unassuming on the hanger in the store, but wearing it, it hugged my curves perfectly. The deep-red color, almost the shade of blood, brought out my green eyes. The neckline scooped a little low, showing a hint of cleavage. And when I walked, it revealed a deep slit that reached the top of my thigh. I had paired them with some strappy black heels, figuring there would be minimal walking involved at this party, so I could power through the night with something a little high on my feet.

My hair was in loose waves, draped over one shoulder. I felt like a bombshell. Shyam hadn't been able to keep his hands off me on the ride here. I knew I'd be going home with him tonight, so I had packed a bag of clothes for tomorrow. He'd seemed glad when I had handed the driver an overnight bag, instead of looking nervous about us getting too close.

I stared at him across the room, talking to some of the other board members. He looked like James Bond in his black Armani suit and crisp white shirt. He was much taller than the other men in the group. Even deep in conversation, he managed to ooze sexiness and confidence.

I studied him as he moved his forefinger to his top lip as if deeply considering what one of the men was saying. His ring shone from a distance. I fingered the necklace he had given me; I hadn't taken it off since. It meant a lot to me that he considered me to be a partner in his search for Tarun.

I suddenly remembered to check the progress of the decryption on my phone. Jai had set up the coordinates to be decrypted using the most common method of decryption. He assumed that Tarun would have used symmetric encryption to encode the coordinates of where the photo of Salena had been taken.

Everyone used symmetric encryption these days. It was more secure, thus making it more difficult to crack. That was why it took a long time for the decryption software to cycle, and it still hadn't found a result. It was virtually impossible to decrypt, even with the most advanced and powerful computers. It could be months before we cracked the coordinates, if at all.

On a whim, I had decided to try an older decryption method from the seventies, one that no one used anymore. It had fallen out of favor in tech security because it could only encrypt small amounts of data. However, the coordinates were small pieces of data, so it was worth a try.

I had set up the software a few days ago, and it had been cycling since. I hadn't bothered with permitting notifications to be sent to Shyam or Jai.

I logged into the app, to check on the status. *No match yet.*

"Bored already?" Jai walked up to me, looking like a model in his suit. His appearance was usually more relaxed than his brother's, as he opted for jeans and t-shirts. Even though he was dressed up tonight, he had kept some of his trademark style—no tie and loosened top buttons.

"No, I was just checking the status on the decryption software," I said, tucking my phone back into my clutch.

"I really doubt *he* would be using older encryption methods, but maybe he's just trying to fuck with us," he said in a low voice so that no one could overhear us.

"Maybe. But I figured it would be practically no effort for us to at least try," I said.

"I agree. Any results yet?"

"Nothing. The cycle has six more hours before it starts over again." At least we would find out soon if it had worked or not.

"That's not long at all. Well, maybe something will surface."

I hoped it would. "What are you doing here, anyway? No cute girls around?" I nudged his arm with my elbow.

"Nah, I can't dip in the company ink," he said, giving me a sly smile.

"Has that ever stopped you before?" He was the biggest playboy, and owning his own company was the biggest playing field he could have asked for.

"Careful. You know who signs your paychecks." He winked at me.

"Richard from Accounting?" I teased.

He pointed at me, flashing his most charming smile. "You're too smart for your own good, Becker. Come dance with me." He extended his open hand to me.

I took him up on his offer. "Sure."

He led me through the crowd to the front of the stage and twirled me around to an upbeat tune. It was fun letting loose with Jai. We had become like family in such a short period of time. He was easy to like.

The song ended and we stood facing the band, clapping.

"Mind if I cut in?" a familiar deep voice asked from behind me. I turned to see the most handsome man in the room grinning at our dance performance.

"Be careful. This one's a wild one." Jai bent over, pretending to catch his breath. "I think I need to rest now."

Shyam slipped his hand around my waist. "I'm familiar with her wildness," he said to his brother.

Locking our hands together, we swayed to the music. The band played a slow, romantic song that matched the energy between us. The entire company was probably looking at us, but I didn't care anymore. It didn't matter what anyone thought. I just wanted to feel this moment—remember it forever.

"You look beautiful tonight," he said in a voice smooth like liquid velvet.

"Back at ya, babe." I winked. He loved whenever I called him by his pet name.

He seemed stunned. "I don't think I've ever been called 'beautiful' before."

"Well, it's about time, because you are. You're an amazing person." I moved closer into him, holding him tighter.

He blinked a few times, as if trying to come up with a response, but stayed silent. My compliment had affected him. I was sure he knew how handsome he was from the way women fawned over him, but I thought he was beautiful inside too.

He spun me and dipped me before pulling me back into his body.

"Everyone's staring at us," I said, looking around the room and noticing pairs of eyes glued to us.

"Let them stare." He was completely unaffected by our growing audience.

"You don't mind that they're seeing their boss get cozy with an employee?" I asked in surprise.

"You're not just an employee to me."

My heart raced hearing his words. I stared deep into his eyes, seeing clearer than I ever had before.

"*Jaan*," he continued, "you are more special to me than an employee. You distract me during the day and make me hungry for more through the night."

He pressed a kiss to my lips. I sighed at his touch, parting my mouth to let him in. He deepened the kiss, tasting my tongue with his. As he pressed himself into me, I felt how much his cock loved our kiss.

"Let's get out of here," he growled.

"But we haven't even had dessert," I whispered, keeping my lips close to his.

"That's exactly what I want to do…at home," he said against my mouth.

I wouldn't turn down hot, steamy sex with a gorgeous man. "Lead the way," I said eagerly.

"Give me five minutes. I need to say goodbye to some people first," he said, pressing another quick kiss to my lips before walking off.

I felt like a giddy teenager with how my belly fluttered in excitement. My body craved sex nightly from this man, and it was ready for it right now.

I pulled my phone out again to check my messages while I waited for him. My decryption app had one notification. *One result found.* I stared at my screen in disbelief. Logically, I knew that this could be a false positive, but there was no way to be certain without checking the details, which I couldn't access from my phone.

I looked across the room. Shyam was busy talking to the head of Research and Development. I could just pop into my office and check the summary details, then return before he ever realized I was gone.

I dropped my phone into my clutch and hurried to the elevators.

"Hey." It was Blake. "Leaving so soon?" I hadn't had a chance to talk to him after my birthday party, so things had been left unresolved.

"Hey," I said. "How have you been?" I was nervous to speak to him.

"Good." He stuffed his hands into his pockets. He seemed just as nervous as I was. "Busy with the holidays. I'm going back home this weekend for three weeks."

"Oh…nice." We stood in silence for some time, unsure of what to say to each other next.

God, this is so awkward. "Blake," I said, having decided to address the tension first. "I'm really sorry about the other night."

His shoulders relaxed with relief that I had addressed the awkwardness. "Don't apologize. I just didn't know you were seeing Mr. Sethi."

I didn't reply. What could I say? *Yes, I'm fucking your boss. Sorry to keep it from you.*

"You seem really into each other," he continued. "I wouldn't have come on so strong if I knew."

"I'm sorry I didn't say anything, but to be honest, I didn't know what to say since it's such a recent thing."

"Well, whatever it is seems serious, judging from the way he looks at you. If you're happy, then I'm happy for you. No hard feelings." The softness in his eyes and smile on his lips let me know his feelings were genuine.

I returned the smile. I was glad we had cleared the air to maintain a friendship. He was a sweet person and would no doubt find a great girl one day.

"Were you going somewhere just now?" he asked.

Our conversation had distracted me from my mission. "Oh, yeah, I just wanted to check on something in my office."

"Forever the hardest worker at the company. They should pay you overtime."

"If only!" I laughed. "Hey, let's get together after you come back from California?"

"That sounds great. Happy holidays, Amelia."

"Happy holidays!" I said, before rushing off to the elevators.

I rode the elevator alone. No one at the party cared about work tonight. They were all too many glasses of champagne in to care about anything work related, so there was no one on the higher floors.

I ran into my office, keeping the door open and the lights off since it would only take me a couple of minutes to check the report and the light from the hallway was enough for me to see. I logged into my computer and loaded the software.

"Come on," I whispered impatiently as the results loaded.

When they finally appeared on the monitor, they showed coordinates of *26.9124° N, 75.7873° E*. I entered them into Google. *Jaipur, India.* I looked at the map and saw that it was southwest of the capital of New Delhi. And close to Shyam's base in Punjab. Salena had been there. But had Tarun been there too? He must have been, right? He would be with his fiancée, even if he were forcing her to marry him.

Another notification popped up on my screen. It was from the facial-recognition software. A match had been found to one of the pictures stored on the cloud. I clicked the alert and the program opened. The photo of Salena in her engagement outfit loaded from our shared cloud. I had seen the picture before, but it was still difficult to see a woman with eyes so dead. Her outfit was beautiful, and her jewelry was impeccable, but she looked like a ghost. It was so eerie that it gave me chills. My heart broke for her, even though she was my Shyam's ex-girlfriend. No woman deserved to be treated the way she had.

Bright blue arrows outlined a spot on the glass window behind her. *What?* Why would the glass trigger a match? The software was usually accurate if it found a match. I was confused.

I zoomed in on the area that was highlighted. It looked like a smear on the glass. I zoomed in even further.

"Fuck!" I gasped. A face. It was a man. I pulled up the photo that it was being compared to by the software. It was one of the ones I had altered of Tarun's brother, stripped of his prosthetics. The reflection in the window had a face like Vik's, but it was thinner and had hollow cheeks. Was this Tarun? It had to be either Vik himself or a relative for it to be a match. A large dark spot was visible on the neck of the person. A birthmark. I pulled up the old photo of Tarun, where he was chubbier. His neck had a large brown birthmark. *It's him!*

I had to tell Shyam. I grabbed my phone to send him a text.

Just then, large hands grabbed my waist from behind and covered my mouth. I thrashed my body around to free myself, but I couldn't break loose. I tried to scream, but no sound came out.

"Boss didn't tell me you'd have such a tight little body," a raspy voice hissed into my ear. Its owner had a thick Indian accent. Hot breath blew on my neck. "Maybe he wouldn't mind if I tried out this cunt before I deliver you."

The monster used the hand that was on my waist to grope my vagina through my dress. Tears poured from my eyes. I tried to push away from him, but he was too strong for me.

"Stay still, sweetheart. You're going to like this." I could feel his hard-on press into my back. I wanted to vomit and pass out all at the same time. This couldn't be happening to me again. I remembered from the time I had been mauled at Nirvana that the element of surprise was how Shyam had defended me. I bit down hard on my attacker's hand until I was rewarded with the metallic taste of his blood. He cursed and let go of me in surprise.

"Fucking bitch!"

I screamed and ran around the desk, and the bottom of my dress caught on its metal leg. I stumbled toward the door and ran into a hard chest that felt like a wall. I fell backward onto the floor.

Another man hovered over me, holding a gun pointed at my chest. His smile was gnarly, and his neck and arms were covered in tattoos. He looked familiar. *At the bar.* He was one of the men who'd been sitting at the bar that night I was with Nat, before I had gone home with Shyam for the first time.

I inched back further into the room, away from him.

"You're going to be a challenging one, huh?" He laughed like a maniac. He had an accent too. He grabbed my ankle and yanked hard, pulling me closer to him. I screamed again, hoping someone would be able to hear me. He flipped me over onto my stomach and held my back down with his knee. Terror spread through my body.

I felt a quick pinch in my neck. Confusion made me turn my head back to see what had caused it. The last image I saw was of the giant beast pinning me down, before everything went black.

XXX. Shyam

I couldn't find Amelia. I had left her for a few minutes to wish some of my employees well before they left for the holidays. I usually hated these formalities, but it was important to maintain a good relationship with my board members to ensure they continued to do a good job. If I wanted Sethi Tech to remain the top tech company in the world, then I needed to make sure my employees felt appreciated.

She had been waiting by the Christmas tree for me. I tried texting and calling her phone multiple times, but no answer. I was worried. She knew how important it was to me that she answered my calls.

I found Jai surrounded by a group of female new hires. The women hung on his every word, laughing every so often at jokes he told—likely stupid jokes. I tore him away from his harem and asked him if he had seen her.

"I haven't seen her since I danced with her," he said.

"Shit." I grabbed my hair in frustration. Where could she be?

"What's wrong?" he asked, growing more concerned.

"She's not answering her phone." I checked my phone again to make sure I hadn't missed her calls or texts in the meantime.

"Well, maybe she just stepped out to get some air?" he suggested.

"It's freezing outside." It was too cold for her to have been waiting outside.

"Good point. Let's get security to see if they can find her. And we'll get Saran to help if she really is missing." Jai took out his phone and called Saran to fill him in on the situation and tell him to stand by.

I was on my way to talk to the security guard monitoring the party when I bumped into that dipshit who had been trying to hit on Amelia at her birthday. I hadn't even seen him.

I wasn't planning on apologizing because I had a bigger problem on my hands, but he stopped me to talk. *Fucking hell.*

"Oh, hey, Mr. Sethi. Sorry about bumping into you."

I kept walking, ignoring him.

He was really shitty at taking a hint, so he kept talking. "Are you okay? You seem to be in a rush like Amelia was. Is something happening?"

I turned back around and approached him, hovering over him. "You saw her?" I demanded.

He backed up, scared by my tone. "Yeah, she was on her way up to her office. Something about checking on work stuff."

"How long ago was this?" I lowered my face in front of his and studied his eyes. It was a habit I had attained from interrogating traitors.

Blake drew his eyes to the ground to avoid my stare. "About thirty minutes ago," he answered quickly to get me to leave him alone.

I ran to the elevator and took it all the way up to our floor. I ran to her office. The lights were off, and it looked empty. I hit the light switch, illuminating the room. I saw her phone on the floor behind her desk. I picked it up and found all my messages and calls on her lock screen. She had never received them. Her computer was locked. Why had she been up here?

I noticed something else by my foot. I bent down to the floor by the leg of her desk. Just then, Jai showed up in the doorway. "What is it?"

My heart pounded so hard in my chest that I couldn't hear anything. Time slowed as I held up the red scrap of fabric. *Her dress.*

"Tarun has her." My voice was broken with panic.

XXXI. Amelia

Everything was blurry. I blinked quickly to clear my vision. I was lying on something that felt like it was moving. I tried to sit up, but my hands were bound together under my stomach. I used my hands to press into the cushion I was lying on. My head pounded.

I looked around to get my bearings. I was in the back seat of a car. My memory came rushing back to me when I saw the man sitting across from me. He was the one who had flipped me over in my office. He stared me in my eye, warning me to sit still, with his gun fixed in my direction.

"Where are you taking me?" My voice was hoarse. I was afraid of saying something that might cause him to pull the trigger.

"You'll see," he said gruffly. I was betting I wasn't going to get anything more out of him without pissing him off.

I looked out the window to see if I could figure it out myself. The sky seemed hazy like there was tons of smog in the air. The street was filled with people walking or riding on bikes with carriages. I saw cows with horns walking down the street too. The buildings seemed old and ornate. Women in colorful outfits and bracelets shopped at vendors outside and men in shirts and cotton skirts prepared food in street carts. I was in India. *Holy shit.*

After some time, the car stopped abruptly. I was grateful because the bumpy roads had been making me want to throw up and I was sure my captor wouldn't have appreciated that.

The car door opened, and the man pulled me out of the car by the chains on my hands. The metal cut into my flesh, causing me to cry out.

"*Chup*. Shut up, you stupid bitch. Get up." I stood as best I could. He pressed the end of the barrel into my back. "Walk."

The air was so heavy and thick that it suffocated me. My body broke out into a sweat immediately under the fabric of my evening gown, but I couldn't tell if it was from the humidity or the adrenaline.

We walked up a pathway to a big pink building. It looked almost like a castle. Men with rifles lined the stairs to the front door. I hesitated before taking the first step. My captor didn't like that much and hit me with the butt of his gun on the back of my head. My eyes teared up in reflex.

"That's no way to treat our guest, Motu." A short man with sunken eyes and hollow cheekbones stood in the doorway at the top of the steps. His neck was covered by that familiar misshapen brown mark. *Tarun.*

"Come inside. You must be tired from your travels." He motioned me inside, as if I had a choice to enter. I followed his order and walked into the colorfully tiled foyer. A fountain stood in the middle to show off the grandness of the room.

"Welcome to my home, Amelia." He stood in front of me, dressed in an Indian jacket made of colorful patches covered in embroidery, which made him look like that maniac from the Batman comics. He was just missing the clown makeup and green hair.

"How do you know my name?" My voice came out shaky, revealing my fear.

"I know everything about you and what you do. We have a—*friend* in common," he said, as if we were at a dinner party making small talk.

"I don't know why you would need me. I'm no one of interest." Tears threatened to fall from the corners of my eyes.

He stepped closer to me, leaning his face closer to mine to look into my eyes. I could smell his rank breath. "Quite the contrary. You are valuable to my friend; therefore, you are *unbelievably valuable* to me."

"Please, let me go. I won't tell anyone where you are or what happened to me." I just wanted to go home and end this nightmare.

"Lying to your host is not the best way to start off your vacation, Amelia," he said, raising his hands in a flourish. I noticed a ring similar to the one Shyam wore, but with a tiger on it.

He studied my face. "I can see why he has kept you a secret. You really are a rare gem with such beautiful red hair. Like a ruby," he said as he pulled a lock of my hair between his fingers and rubbed it. His lizard-like eyes raked down my body, taking in my revealing outfit. When he raised his eyes again, they settled on my neck.

"That's a beautiful necklace you have. It looks like something I've seen before." He lifted the pendant with his fingers to examine it.

Oh no.

He yanked the chain off my neck, causing me to yelp. "And you say you're no one of interest. You're perhaps the most *interesting* person I've met so far." Holding out the necklace, he turned to Motu and said, "Send this to our friend, Shyam. I trust you remember where he works. He'll know what it means."

Motu took it from his hands and scurried away.

Tarun turned away from me and issued one last command to his men before walking away. "Show our guest to her cell."

Suddenly, I was yanked away from the foyer by two armed guards.

XXXII. Shyam

I sat in my suite at Nirvana, a broken man. I had closed the club since Amelia went missing so I could use it for privacy. I hadn't gone home or even slept in four days. I still wore my suit from the holiday party. My stomach was empty except for copious amounts of scotch.

How had this happened? Security had been so tight. Not even our cameras had caught footage of Amelia being taken.

I kept playing all the terrible things that they could have done to her in my mind and it made me sick.

This couldn't be happening again. First my mother, then Salena, and now Amelia.

Jai had searched her computer and found that she had found a hit with the decryption algorithm she was running, and a reflection we suspected to be Tarun's. I had had my men in India scour the city of Jaipur, but Tarun had given us general coordinates for the city, so we didn't have a specific location of where Amelia might be. It was possible that she wasn't in Jaipur at all. She could be anywhere.

My brilliant Amelia. Why did I get her involved? I regretted ever hiring her and forcing her to take on such a dangerous mission because of my need for revenge.

Jai entered my office. I didn't even bother looking up to acknowledge him.

"We'll find her." He tried to sound reassuring, but I heard the doubt in his voice. "She's tough and smart. She'll survive this."

I hoped to God he was right.

"The guys have the city covered. Zayn says that all men involved in surveillance have been shown photos of what she looks like. She'll stand out easily in India. Someone will find her," he continued to console me.

A million thoughts raced through my head. I'd have given anything just to have her with me—safe. It was my job to protect her and I had failed.

Javed stalked into my office. "This just arrived. We suspect it's from Tarun." He held a small box in his hand.

I stood up and approached him slowly. I didn't want to open the box because I knew nothing good could come of it. But I had to know what was inside.

I took it from him. Slowly, I lifted the lid. *Amelia's necklace.*

The black diamond eyes glistened as I rubbed my fingers along the pendant, as if they were trying to tell me of the dangers it had seen when she had still been wearing it. The chain was broken, as if it had been ripped off her neck.

I had once done this same thing with Tarun's brother's ring. He had sent me a message that only I would understand.

I fell to my knees, letting the box fall to the floor. My hands covered my eyes as I let out a howl of agony. The pain cut me deep through my heart. I felt like I was bleeding out on the floor.

I pulled my hands from my eyes and stared vacantly, my vision blurring as moisture rolled down my face. Nothing mattered anymore. She was dead, and now I was dead too.

Thank you so much for reading POWER! I had a great time creating Shyam and Amelia's story. It was exciting for me to feature a heroine that worked in the tech field which is usually male-dominated. I loved exploring each character and seeing how they developed at lovers and partners.

If you enjoyed Part 1 of their story, I'd love to read your review and hear your thoughts.

Stay tuned for Book Two: EMPOWERED to read the thrilling conclusion to Shyam and Amelia's adventure. It will take you on a much-needed ride especially during these times when travel is difficult for all of us. I'm excited to share it with you because I really love the journey this couple takes and how much they grow as individuals, too.

For release updates and previews of new releases, sign up for my mailing list at www.victoriawoodsauthor.com. Also, follow me on Instagram at http://www.instagram.com/victoriawoodsauthor.

Made in the USA
Middletown, DE
10 January 2021